*To the memory of my grandparents,
Nathan Louis Paves, Fanny Paves,
Joseph Yashinsky and Dinah Blank*

Contents

Reaching Across

Maximum Nightmare

Bonestories

Introduction

All my life I've been haunted by a story. My grandfather used to tell it to me when I was young. It is about something that happened to him many years ago, at the beginning of the twentieth century. He had left Romania, travelled the world, and was living in San Francisco, California, at the time. One night he had a dream. He saw his grandfather walking toward him, his body filled with light. His grandfather, radiant, spoke to him in a kindly voice: "I've come to say goodbye, Nick, and to tell you I love you very much." So saying, he disappeared. In the morning my grandfather remembered his dream. He wrote it in his diary; then he wrote a letter back to Bucharest, asking for news. He knew his grandfather had emigrated from Romania to St. Louis, Missouri, but he didn't have his current address. The letter took a long time going — this was before e-mail, fax, phone or airplanes — and the reply took a long time coming. When he finally received a letter, it contained sad news. His grandfather had died. He remembered his dream. When he looked in his diary, he saw that his grandfather had died on the same day that he had had his dream.

My grandfather, by the way, was an engineer (he specialized in concrete) and an amateur mathematician. He was a man of facts, of numbers, of equations. Yet after this experience, he also became a believer in mysteries, spirits, dreams and ghosts. When he wanted to teach me his belief, he would draw the mathematical sign for infinity — a horizontal figure eight — and explain that every creature had something of infinity within, something that could never die. Maybe that's why he used to treasure and retell his own dream-tale of a beloved grandfather.

Ghostwise is a book of stories that my grandfather would have enjoyed. The stories here are about strange experiences, things beyond the everyday, good ghosts and malevolent phantoms. I call them "midnight" stories. They're meant to be told at a late hour, in a dark room, with a single candle-flame the only light, and with a few friends gathered around to listen.

As in *Next Teller*, my first collection of Canadian storytelling, all the stories in *Ghostwise* are alive and well and living outside the covers of this book. The storytellers who wrote them down also know these tales in their heads. They tell them to listeners across Canada, from Newfoundland to Vancouver Island, from Whitehorse to Toronto. They tell them in kitchens, around campfires, at small-town doughnut shops, at storytelling festivals, in outport cookhouses and at Elders' gatherings — all the places people get together to enjoy word-of-mouth stories. The tales come from many different cultures and traditions: Nootka, Jewish, Chinese, Japanese, Scottish, Irish, Québécois, Jamaican, Tlingit and many others. You'll find many accents and dialects of English in the book. Sharon Shorty's Yukon story has a Tlingit rhythm, and Stanley Sparkes's tale is full of Newfoundland salt. In the Alabama story of Jim Meeks you'll encounter "haints" — Southern talk for ghosts. Some are ancient tales, and some are from today's world. What connects these stories is that all of them have a trace of ghost-wisdom.

There are five sections in Ghostwise: 1. "Heart and Horror," 2. "Shhh...," 3. "Reaching Across," 4. "Maximum Nightmare," 5. "Bonestories." In "Heart and Horror," there are stories about people who encounter such monsters as the Boogie-Woman, the Devil, a ghoulish spider and the dreaded Manananggal. In these stories, heroes — often children — fight the evil creature with a courage they didn't know they possessed. To remind you of how much power your own storytelling can have on the younger members of your family, I've included Chris Lindgren's (mostly) true account of the horror stories she heard from her older sister. Think of "Moans and Groans" the next time you have to babysit.

Sometimes a story leaves you speechless, still looking at the story's mind-movies long after the teller's voice has fallen silent. Those are the stories you'll find in "Shhh..." You'll read about the extraordinary power of dreams, about a fortune-teller in the Second World War, and about a Scottish piper who crosses the threshold of an enchanted cottage. You'll also find a wild Irish tale about a man who thinks he has no stories, until he tumbles down a mysterious well.

"Reaching Across" comes next, with stories about spirits who speak to us across the shifting border that separates the dead from the living. Some are funny, some sad, some true and some made-up. All of them teach us that we're never as far as we think — or hope — from whatever place these spirits inhabit.

If you venture as far as "Maximum Nightmare," you should prepare for the worst. You will not meet harmless, benevolent, cute ghosties here. This is heavy-duty monster territory. A grotesque face in the casement window in a Ukrainian village, a Japanese ghoul on a lonely mountain, a fox fairy who turns vicious, a pack of dogs deliberately starved by a vengeful master. Don't read this section alone at night, and make sure that your kid brother and your little sister are in the other room if you start telling this stuff out loud.

Ghostwise ends with seven "Bonestories." Every story in this section has a body in it. There are some amusing tales here — like the monkey who dresses up in the dead old woman's clothes, or John Tingle's meeting with the Old Woman of the Woods. There are sad tales as well, about parents and children learning the hardest lesson one can ever learn in this world: how to part with those you love. Sometimes hearing a story about a tragic experience is the best medicine for dealing with it. Stories teach us that other people have been to that dark and dreaded place, and returned to tell us about it. The book ends with the storyteller who began it: Johnny Moses tells us a tale from the ancient "dream" time, a story about life and death coming full circle.

In Tolkien's great epic *The Lord of the Rings*, a wise old tree-creature recalls that the ancient earth-people gained their extraordinary power because "they always wanted to talk to everything, the old Elves did." That desire to be in conversation with things, even if they live beyond the visible and everyday world, is what starts the adventures of the people in this book. Sometimes they triumph in the strange worlds they are drawn to by their listening. A Vietnamese hunter hears a snake's cry for help, and so gains miraculous powers; a young Newfoundlander hears his dead father's voice on a foggy ice-floe, and follows it to safety; a brave girl named Ti-Flor hears the warning voices of the Devil's own fiddle-strings, and so saves her village. These people do well because they bring to their listening courage, resourcefulness and high spirits. The less fortunate characters in this book meet very different fates: the voices they follow lead them to a variety of terrifying dooms at the hands of duppies, wendigos, ravening dogs, fox fairies and loup-garous.

My grandfather had something of Tolkien's Elf-people in his blood. He wanted to talk and listen to everything, even if the voice spoke through a dream. I've never forgotten my grandfather's story. It weaves in and out of my mind, often coming at a time when I need reminding of life's mysteries and possibilities. I'm haunted — in the friendliest way, of course — by his remarkable dream-tale. So even though he has been dead for many years (and the grandpa he dreamed of has been gone for more than a century), the story itself has become my grandfather's way to keep talking to me, his only grandchild. And if that's true for my grandpa's story, maybe it's true for all the stories that haunt their way into your memory, murmuring their wisdom when you most need it.

Could it be that all stories are ghost stories?

Dan Yashinsky
Winter/Spring 1997

Heart
& Horror

The Story of the Boogie-Woman

Johnny Moses

This is a story that I used to hear all the time at night. My grandmother always used to tell it. Have you ever heard of a boogie-man? Well, among our people, we have lots of stories about the boogie-man, but we also have lots of stories about the boogie-woman. The boogie-woman is also known as the "basket lady" or "basket ogress," because she carries a big basket on her back.

The boogie-woman is a really big monster. Since she never takes a bath, she smells real bad, and she's got dirt five inches thick all around her body. She has to breathe out of her mouth, because she has black, petrified snot stuck in her nose. She loves to eat children who don't listen to their parents and grandparents.

• • • • •

Long ago, there were twelve children who lived with their grandmother and grandfather. They never listened to their parents or their grandparents. The only one who kind of listened was the hunchback girl.

They were playing outside, and Grandma called them into the house. "Aay, children, come into the house. I've got something to tell you."

All the children came running into the house. Grandma looked at them and said, "You children stink. You smell funny. You'd better take a bath." And the children said, "Whyyyy?"

Grandpa explained, "Do you know why you children have to take a bath? The boogie-woman loves stinky, smelly children. When the wind blows a certain way, it carries the stinky smell of the children way up the big mountain where the boogie-woman lives, and that's how she tracks the children down. She follows the stinky smell down the mountain."

And the children said, "We don't believe in all that old-fashioned stuff!" The only one who kind of listened was the hunchback girl.

The second time, Grandma called them into the house. "Aay, children, come into the house. I've got something to tell you." They all came running into the house. Grandma looked at the children and said, "Why don't you children clean those balls of wax out of your ears and listen to us for a change?"

These children never listened to their parents or grandparents. They never cleaned their ears out, and they had five-inch balls of wax stuffed in their heads. And the children said, "Whyyyyy?"

Grandpa explained, "Do you know why you've got to listen to your parents for a change and clean those balls of wax out of your ears? The boogie-woman loves children who don't listen. She's got a really big mouth, and she'll go right up to your ear and do this — sluurppp! — and suck all the balls of wax and your brains out, and then you won't have to listen to us any more."

And the children said, "We don't believe in all that old-fashioned stuff!" The only one who kind of listened was the hunchback girl.

Finally, the third and last time, Grandma called them into the house. "Aay, children, come into the house. I've got something to tell you." They all came running into the house. Grandma looked at the children and said, "Uuucch! Why don't you children clean that snot off your nose and chin that's hanging down. It looks terrible!"

These children never cleaned their noses, and the snot hung all the way down to their knees. When the wind blew, their snot swung back and forth. And the children said, "Whyyyyy?"

Grandpa explained. "Do you know why you've got to clean that snot off your nose and your chin that's hanging down, swinging all over the place? The boogie-woman loves snotty children. She loves to eat children who don't listen to their parents, and she cooks them in a big pot. Do you know what she uses their snot for? She uses it for salt."

And the children said, "We don't believe in all that old-fashioned stuff!" The only one who kind of listened was the hunchback girl.

As they were playing that day, the wind was blowing. It blew the stinky smell of the children way up the big mountain where the boogie-woman lived. The boogie-woman got so excited. She could smell them from miles away. She started climbing down the mountain.

As she walked down the mountain, she breathed out of her mouth. She was carrying that big basket on her back.

When she came out of the bushes and trees, she called to the children.

"Would anybody like some berries?" she asked.

All the children ran to her hand, and they ate these sweet, juicy berries. "Ummmm!" But on her other hand the boogie-woman had sticky stuff called "pitch." She took the pitch and rubbed their faces, and they couldn't see. Then she grabbed each child and threw him over her shoulder into the big basket. Do you know what the children said when they were going into the basket? They said, "Aaaaaaaaah!"

While they were in the basket, the boogie-woman sang her supper song: "I'm gonna eat the little ones. I'm gonna eat the little ones. I'm gonna eat the little ones. I'm gonna eat the little ones."

As she was singing her supper song, the only one who was kind of smart was the hunchback girl. She took the pitch out of her eyes. Then she climbed out of the basket and ran down the mountain, back to the village, to tell the people what had happened.

She said to the people, "The boogie-woman's got all the children, and she's going to eat them!" So the big, strong warriors followed the hunchback girl up the mountain.

When they got up the mountain, they hid behind some bushes and trees. There, the boogie-woman was dancing around the big fire, doing her boogie dance, singing her supper song: "I'm gonna eat the little ones."

While she was singing her supper song, the big, strong warriors took a look at the boogie-woman and they got scared.

They said, "Uhhhh! She's too scary-looking! We can't do anything!"

The hunchback girl got mad. She looked at the strong warriors and she said, "What's the matter with you? You're supposed to be warriors!" She got so mad that she was full of strength. She ran behind the boogie-woman and pushed the boogie-woman into the big fire.

The boogie-woman popped all over, like popcorn, into these little pieces. And some of the pieces turned into the little birds we have today. Her blood went all over, like fireworks, and the drops of her blood still live today. Some people call them the "mosquitoes," because they love your blood.

The little hunchback girl had saved all the children. They all returned to the village, and they all kind of listened to their grandmas and grandpas.

And that is all.

Ti-Flor and the Devil

Chris Cavanagh

Once upon a time, in the early days of Acadia, there was a wee girl named Ti-Flor who was something of a trouble-maker. You could always count on her to do exactly what she was told not to do. At least she was dependable this way.

Now, in those days, life was hard and the people were pious. It is said that the Devil walked the land openly in those times. And if he tricked you, he could take your soul.

Ti-Flor loved one time of the year especially, and that was Mardi Gras, the day before the beginning of the forty days of Lent that would end with Palm Sunday and Easter. Mardi Gras, Fat Tuesday, was a day of celebration, and all the villages of Acadia held wonderful parties.

Not all the villages were lucky enough to have their own musicians. The village where Ti-Flor lived didn't even have a fiddler. Well, Ti-Flor decided to see to that. Even though she had been told never, never to go out of the village, she snuck away and went to crossroads where people met and gossiped.

Careful to stay hidden, she would listen to the old men and women, and soon she heard what she needed. Some of the old folks spoke of a fiddler who was still looking for a town to play in. It was said that he wore a most wonderful scarf, long and wrapped many times round his neck, and that it had all the colours of the rainbow in it.

Ti-Flor began to search. Each day she would sneak out of her village and go to a different crossroad. It was on Tuesday morning of Mardi Gras that she spotted the fiddler people had spoken of. Sure enough, his scarf waved in the wind and had in it all the colours of the rainbow. Ti-Flor, bold as could be, walked right up to that fiddler and asked if he would play for her village. The fiddler smiled a big smile and said, "Sure!"

Ti-Flor marched triumphantly into town with the fiddler at her side, ready to receive the praise and thanks she knew she deserved. All she got was a scolding for having left the village. The villagers were happy enough to see a fiddler come to their town, but Ti-Flor was told to stay with the other children in a house near the church, where they would spend the night while the adults danced.

Dance until midnight, that is. For everyone knew that Mardi Gras ended at midnight and any who partied past midnight risked having the Devil take their souls. Of course, no one in the village worried about that since all knew what fine people they were.

Ti-Flor was upset that she was not thanked, and all the more angry for being locked up with all the other children. She would not stand for that and, true to her nature, snuck out of the house and made her way over to the church to watch the preparations.

She was about to walk around the church when she noticed the fiddler, wrapped up in his scarf, sitting on a bench against the church wall. Ti-Flor decided not to disturb him. After all she might be found out and sent back to the house. The fiddler was plucking at the strings of his fiddle, when one broke. He pulled the broken strands off, reached into a small pouch about his waist and drew out a shiny new string. He strung it onto the fiddle and was tuning it up when a second sting snapped. Again he reached into the pouch for a new string. As he tightened it onto the fiddle, the third one snapped. He looked annoyed as he tugged this last string away from the fiddle and replaced it from the pouch. He tightened and tuned his three strings, played a few notes and seemed pleased with the results. Before Ti-Flor could surprise him from her hiding place, the fiddler collected his things, got up from the bench and went around the corner to go into the church. Ti-Flor noticed something glittering on the ground by the bench.

When she looked closer she saw the three broken strings. And they seemed to gleam golden in the light of the setting sun. When she picked them up, she was sure that they were made of gold. They were smooth and cool to her touch.

She heard her name called and turned around quickly to see who had found her. There was no one there. Again she heard her name being spoken. She listened hard, and then realized with a shock that the sound was coming from the golden strings she held in her hand. She was a bit afraid, but that had never stopped her before. She held the strings closer to her face.

"Ti-Flor, Ti-Flor," the strings said, "you are in great danger. You must stop him."

"Who are you?" Ti-Flor asked.

"We are the souls of people whom the Devil has tricked. For the fiddler you have brought to your town is the Devil himself. Tonight, the Devil will play his fiddle, but that is no ordinary fiddle. When he plays, it is impossible not to dance. He plans to play past midnight. Then the souls of your village will be his to take."

Ti-Flor was horrified to realize that she was the one who had brought the Devil to their town. If any lost their souls, it would be her fault. "But how can I stop him," she asked the strings. "I'm just a little girl."

"There is one way to break his spell. When midnight approaches, you must throw us under his feet while he dances and plays. When he steps on us, the magic spell will be broken. You will know when it is time."

Ti-Flor knew what she had to do. Although she was afraid, she also knew that she had caused this terrible situation. She was determined to set things right.

Careful, so as to let no one see her, she snuck into the church and hid in a corner. The fiddler began to play. His scarf flowed about his head like a cloud of colour, and Ti-Flor could see the magic at work. Everyone was dancing, but none of them seemed to notice that they had no choice but to dance when the music played. They said to each other that they had never heard such beautiful music. And Ti-Flor, protected from the magic by the strings she held, also had to admit that she had never heard such beautiful music.

Midnight was approaching, and although all of them looked exhausted, still they danced. Ti-Flor looked at the dancers and saw that none of them were touching the ground.

And they seemed to be rising higher as she watched. She knew that it must be midnight. She crept out of her hidden corner and made her way carefully to within reach of the fiddler. The Devil was dancing and laughing and playing his fiddle while his scarf of many colours moved in time to the music.

He jumped up and Ti-Flor threw the strings under his feet. When the Devil stepped on the strings, he screamed as though he had stepped on knives. He stopped playing for a second and the spell was broken. All the dancers thumped onto the floor. In that moment, they knew what had happened and how close they had come to losing their souls. They saw Ti-Flor standing at the front of the church and they knew who their saviour had been.

Everyone turned to look at the fiddler, who was still playing, although the magic had been broken. It was now the fiddler who was floating above the floor, and every second he rose higher. All the while he continued to play. Everyone still had to admit that it was the most beautiful music they had ever heard.

At first it looked as if the fiddler would bump into the roof, but he passed right on through. Everyone ran outside and, sure enough, there was the fiddler floating right above the church, his scarf waving its colours across that night sky. He looked down, and saw Ti-Flor looking back up at him. He smiled and winked at her. Then he floated right up into that night sky, playing his fiddle all the while, until all that could be seen of him was his scarf. Those colours danced across that sky just as they do to this day. And we call them the "Northern Lights."

And they say that when the Northern Lights dance across the sky, if you listen really hard, you can hear that fiddler playing still.

The Other Way Home

Dennis Mann

"**B**all hog!" That's what Nick and Scott had called me. They said I didn't pass the soccer ball to them enough.

We had walked to the park together after dinner for soccer practice, but now I was mad and I wasn't going to walk home with them. Mom had said we had to stay together and come home before it got dark. Well, I knew a way to get home before dark and still not walk with them.

I was going to go out through the fence at the back of the park and along the railway tracks. That was a shortcut that my grandpa and I sometimes used when he came for a visit.

He'd tell my mom and dad we were going to look for treasures. Sometimes we brought stuff back. I liked those trips because he would tell me stories as we walked, and he'd get me to tell him stuff too. Each time we got back, he would make me promise never, never, never to go there unless I was with either him or my father. He'd say, "It's no place for a kid to go, if he wants to grow up."

Now I was older and mad at Scott and Nick, and the tracks were the fastest way home. And I had to be home before dark.

I heard the train noise just after I climbed through the fence and started to walk along the tracks. I moved off the tracks to watch the train pass. Instead the train stopped. I stayed well back. I'd heard lots of stories about kids being killed or crippled around trains.

I finally realized that I had better start moving or I'd be late getting home. I jumped across the ditch at the edge of the tracks and walked along the fence between the buildings and the tracks. I went slowly at first because the path was full of junk and weeds and brush. After a while, the train whistle blew and the train started moving. It was moving so slowly that I was keeping up with it and at the same time staying close to the fence.

It was hard to walk along the fence line, so after the train passed I crossed over the ditch again and started to walk along the edge of the tracks. It was easier, but the big stones made it hard to walk in my soccer boots. That's when I realized that I'd left my running shoes at the park. I thought about going back for them, but realized that it was getting dark, and I knew my mother would be starting to worry.

I continued walking along the edge of the track. I thought about other trips in the area and tried to recognize some of the buildings and things my grandfather called "landmarks." It was getting so dark I could hardly tell what I was seeing. I thought more about my grandpa and the stories he told. There were lots of things going on in my head.

I was sure my mom and dad would be out looking for me by now. All I wanted to see were the streetlights on the road I knew had to be ahead. I walked for a long time, tripping over those big rocks beside the tracks. Then I stopped and thought I had better make a plan. That's what Grandpa always said: "Bad things happen when people don't have a plan." I also remembered one time he said, "If you're ever caught out at night away from home, do what the animals do. Don't travel; find a safe place and go to ground. Hold up someplace 'til it's daylight. Then, if you know where you're going, it'll be safe to move around again. But if you're lost, just stay put."

A whole lot of stuff I had been told came back to me. I wanted to remember it all. All the stuff people and books told you to do when you're lost in a strange place. I tried to make a plan. But at the same time I was thinking that Nick and Scott would be home by now. They had probably had a snack and were in bed. This was what Grandpa meant when he said, "Make sure you don't sacrifice judgment for pride." Maybe I was too tired and hungry to think right. Maybe I'd got turned around and was in a place I had never been before. I realized the bit of light I had was from the moon. It was definitely time for me to look for a safe place to "go to ground."

That's when I noticed something familiar. It was hard to be sure in the dark, but it looked like a short bit of road that ran past a small grey building near a hole in the fence. I was sure that I'd been there before. Grandpa had called it a "gatehouse." I went over to the little building. The windows were boarded up, and the door was broken and kind of half open. I looked inside and, from what I could see, it looked the same as it had when Grandpa and I had peered in. Lots of spider webs, some writing on the walls, and the floor littered with rocks from the tracks and with broken glass. I moved inside and noticed a giant spider web in one corner. I walked to the far corner away from the door and the spider web, and kicked some stuff around on the floor to make a place to sit down. Then I sat with my back to the wall, facing the door and the spider web. That's when I realized how tired I was.

I felt pretty safe, but at the same time I knew that everyone would be worried and looking for me. I guess I must have dropped off to sleep, because I remember waking up thinking someone was near me. I looked around, but all I could see was the square of moonlight on the dirty floor. The moon seemed brighter than it had been and I could see more of the room although there wasn't anything more in the room to see. The spider web was bigger than I'd thought at first. I listened for a while to see if I could hear anyone calling my name. Nothing. I didn't have any idea of the time but remembered Grandpa saying a good sleep was the best way to hurry the dawn. I tried to sleep, but it was hard to stop thinking about home.

I guess I must have dropped off to sleep again, because I remember waking up lying flat out on the floor. I sensed that I was not alone in the room. I tried to see what was there. From the way my clothes were shifted I thought something might have dragged me onto the floor. I could vaguely remember being pulled along as I slept. Was that what woke me up? Was I imagining things because I hadn't eaten and was tired? Grandpa said that could happen sometimes.

I moved back up against the wall and stared around the room slowly, examining everything carefully. There seemed to be something over by the spider web. I could see through it — or thought I could. It was a yellowish-green cloud about the size of my little sister. It wasn't standing on the floor but seemed to be floating above it. Below it I could see something black and white on the floor. I don't know why, but I looked down at my feet, and my left soccer shoe was gone. I was imagining things. I must have kicked the shoe off while I was sleeping. I decided that I wouldn't go to sleep again.

I waited and watched for a long time, but nothing happened. I was getting tired again. My eyes would close for a minute and my head would jerk me back awake.

I shook myself hard to wake up. There really was something there. The yellowish-green cloud was closer, just on the other side of the bit of moonlight on the floor. It had more shape than before, like a small person or upright animal. I could make out a head above the body. If it had a mouth, it seemed to be sneering at me. There were no teeth, just a long snout and a tongue that I thought I could see flicking in and out. I bit my lip, to be sure I wasn't dreaming. It hurt.

Somehow, I knew that this thing was like the wild animals that Grandpa talked about. It was afraid of the light. That's why it didn't come any closer. It wouldn't pass that bar of moonlight on the floor. I would be safe as long as the moon shone through the door. I relaxed. I was safe for the time being. I had to make a plan.

Grandpa had said, never turn your back on danger. Don't run. Stand and face trouble down. Most predators attack from the back. If the prey doesn't turn and run, predators don't attack. Try not to let anything get hold of your hands or legs; keep them protected. Use a rock or a stick to keep the attacker a distance away from you. If you have to strike out, move fast and hard with no warning, and that will usually scare off anything that threatens you. I tried to come up with a plan that would do all the things Grandpa had said. When I looked up again, the thing had moved.

It was now closer to the light. A piece of rope — or maybe its tongue — flicked at my leg and foot, trying to get hold of me. When the thing realized I was awake, it stopped. It seemed to talk to me — not with sound, but right into my brain. It told me to come over to that side of the room. I would be safe, and there was water and food for me if I wanted it.

"No!" I yelled.

The sound of my voice seemed to scare it, and it jumped back in surprise. It was afraid of noise; at least I knew that now. I decided to keep on talking, maybe even sing to keep it back. I sang the few songs I knew and recited the rhymes I could remember. It worked. The thing stayed back, moving its head from side to side as if it was trying to understand. I never knew before how tiring singing and talking in a loud voice can be. I sure wished I knew more songs and rhymes, because after a few minutes I couldn't remember any more stuff to say.

I guess it didn't really matter, because by the time I stopped singing it had moved closer to the light again. Again the rope or tongue seemed to be trying to get hold of my leg. Each time it flicked out, I'd move, but I was getting tired of watching for it and moving just enough for it to miss me. After one of the moves I found my hand was touching one of those big rocks from beside the tracks. I picked it up.

Now the thing was trying real hard to get hold of me. I remember thinking that it had to get me before daylight. If it was in a hurry, maybe daylight was coming soon. I had to find a way to hang tough, as Grandpa would say.

I guess I made the mistake of moving the same way each time the tongue or rope came at me. I remember the coach saying if you do the same thing every time you get the ball, the defenders will learn how to stop you. I should have remembered that. The next time the thing tried to catch me, it faked the move. I moved quickly, but before I got settled it flicked its tongue out for real and caught my foot.

The thing didn't pull me back quickly. I guess I was pretty heavy for something its size. I just found myself being dragged slowly across the floor. It was time to strike out hard and fast with no warning. I knew that if I was going to throw the rock hard and be sure to hit the target, I had to be on my feet. In one quick movement I rolled toward the thing and jumped to my feet. I threw the rock as hard as I could.

Before I could see what happened, I was pulled onto the floor again. I think I must have hit the floor hard, because I don't remember anything for a while.

When I came back to my senses, I was lying on the floor quite a ways from the wall. I looked around and couldn't see the thing. I crawled to my corner and put my back against the wall. I examined the room closely, but I still couldn't see the thing. Was it gone? Had it been there at all? Had I dreamed all this? I wasn't going to take any chances. I sat upright and kept watch. After some time I noticed the moonlight on the floor was fading. Grandpa always said it got darker before the dawn, so I figured first light must be coming soon. I was now sure I had dreamed the whole thing and began to relax.

I guess I must have dropped off to sleep again, because the next thing I remember was a voice saying, "Nathan, Nathan. Is your name Nathan?" When I opened my eyes, it was light and I was staring at a big black boot. There was a blue pant leg with a red stripe above it.

"Yes, my name is Nathan and I'm okay," I said. I thought she'd want to know I was okay. I was big for my age, but she reached down and picked me up in her arms like a baby. At first I didn't like it and tried to get free, but she held tight and kept saying, "Yes, you're okay, yes, you're okay."

As we started out of the building and along the path and train tracks to the police car, I felt safe in her arms. She talked on the radio in the car. She and another police officer she called Russ asked me a bunch of questions. I didn't tell them about my dream, but I did tell them everything else. They said they were going to take me home so that I could have a bath and something to eat. They said they'd be back to talk to me after I had some sleep. That sounded good to me.

When the police officer was making sure my seatbelt was on, he said, "Where's your other shoe?" I'd forgotten about it. I told him it was back in the building. He said we'd go find it together.

We started back along the tracks with me holding his arm and kind of hopping. We had no trouble finding the soccer boot, and I sat down on the floor to put it on while he looked around the little shack I had spent the night in.

"Look at the size of that spider web," he said. "I don't like spiders. I don't think I could have spent the night in here."

I looked and was surprised that the web took up the entire corner of the room and halfway along each wall. I hadn't seen it in daylight before. It was sure the biggest web I had ever seen until then or since. I finished putting my shoe on and stood up to head for the door. The police officer was ahead of me.

As I walked, I noticed the big rock on the floor and kicked it with my foot. At the place where the rock had been, there was a big, yellow-green oozing glob. The policeman looked back at it, too.

"Even squashed and dead, that has to be the biggest spider I have ever seen," he said.

I nodded but couldn't say anything. I just wanted out of there fast.

Everyone who'd spent the night looking for me was waiting when I got home. They were all happy to see me and carried on about how lucky I was. I knew better. If I'd done what I said I was going to do, none of this would have happened. As Grandpa often said, I was the author of my own misfortune. I told Grandpa about parts of the night, about making a plan and going to ground and the stuff like that. He rubbed my head and said "You did good, boy." That made me feel better.

I never told anyone before about the yellowish-green thing, partly because part of me thinks I was dreaming. But there is another part of me that wonders how I could take so long to walk a block along that train track. Why couldn't I see the lights on the road ahead of me? It was and still is only about two soccer fields between those two roads. Where did the time go? Where did I go? When I think about these things, I know it's true; but nobody would want to believe it, including me.

The Manananggal

Cynthia Goh

I grew up on a remote island in the tropics. Every night at about six o'clock, all year round, the sun went down in a blaze of red and orange that spread across the sky. Within minutes the only light left was from the moon, the stars, and the kerosene lamps casting long shadows away from the houses.

At six o'clock, the church bells rang for the Angelus; at six o'clock, work ended for the day; at six o'clock, we kids stopped playing with our friends and went home. My grandfather closed up his store, and everybody sat around outside. The men drank beer and ate dried anchovies and waited for dinner, passing the time, joking and laughing and talking about their day and, best of all, telling stories.

Friday nights were the best time. There was no school the next day, so we kids were allowed to stay up and listen to the stories for as long as we liked. I'd stay for hours. If I waited long enough, I knew that Mamang, my grandmother and the matriarch of the family, would start to tell us about her days growing up in a village far away across the island. Her village was so small that it made our little town seem like a bustling city, and so far away that nobody else in town had ever been there. But we knew it must be an interesting place, from Mamang's stories. They certainly had no shortage of *aswang* there; no one in town knew as much about dealing with the creatures of the night as Mamang.

It was a Friday night when I was introduced to one of the most frightful of the *aswang*, the manananggal. Mamang told us that the manananggal is a young, beautiful woman, with jet-black hair flowing down her back and an hourglass figure with a narrow waist. When it grows dark she twists around and around on her narrow waist until she splits herself into two, a top and a bottom half. Black wings sprout from the top half and she flies off to search for food. If she flies across the moon, she casts a shadow like a huge bat. She especially likes to come out, Mamang added, on Friday nights. My brothers and sisters and I huddled together and looked around nervously.

The bottom half stays behind, just standing there hidden among the banana trees. If you are foolish enough to go out wandering around at night, Mamang said you must carry a handful of salt or ashes. If you come upon the bottom half of a manananggal, you should sprinkle the salt or ashes on it, to prevent the two halves from joining again before sunrise. If the manananggal is caught by the light while it is still split, it will wither away to ashes.

"That's mean," my brother whispered to me.

"Shh!" I hissed.

But Mamang had heard. "Mean? Do you know what the manananggal eats? Her favourite food is … babies!"

She told us that the manananggal has a very long tongue which she can stretch out longer and longer, until it's no thicker than a piece of string. The tongue rolls out, and she sends it searching, searching everywhere for a baby. When she finds one, she sticks her tongue into the baby's navel, and she sucks the life right out.

"Mean? Hah!" Mamang sniffed. She went back inside.

That night, as I went in to our house, I was surrounded by bamboo. The slats of bamboo that formed the floor were a good inch apart. The roof was coconut leaves, the walls were flattened bamboo. Everywhere there were holes and spaces, and windows kept wide open. When it was hot — which was all the time — all these holes served to give good ventilation and help keep us cool in the house. But they weren't much good for protection from a manananggal.

As I was about to settle in for the night, I heard a little gurgling sigh, and looked over at my youngest sister. She was just seven months old and sleeping under the mosquito net. Seven months! Did that mean she was still a baby? I was sure, come to think of it, that my mother had called her a "little baby" just earlier that day. She was small and pink and chubby. Perfect food for the manananggal!

Of course, that made me too worried to go to sleep. I searched the whole bedroom I shared with all my brothers and sisters, looking at all the gaps where a tongue might try to sneak its way in, coming after my little baby sister. Could I seal up all the cracks? No, there were just too many. How could I protect her? I looked at the mosquito netting, and over at the dresser where a bottle of my mother's clear nail polish was sitting ...

"Chi Chi! What are you doing?" my mother shouted when she came into the room.

I was busy sealing up the holes in the mosquito net, using the nail polish. I explained this proudly; I imagined that my mother would congratulate me on my plan.

She didn't. "For heaven's sake, you're going to suffocate her!"

I hadn't known that the holes in mosquito nets were there to let air in. I'd assumed they were there to let you see through, so I was feeling rather clever for choosing the clear nail polish instead of the red one!

I needed to find another way to foil the manananggal. I wandered around, keeping a sharp eye out, not knowing quite what I was looking for or what to do when I found it. Pulling hard on the tongue ought to at least discourage the monster, I decided. After all, I wouldn't much like it if someone yanked on *my* tongue!

What was that, dangling from the table? I gave it a good, hard pull. A bunch of vegetables thumped off the table and onto the floor; I'd grabbed the cord that tied them. What was that black thing, coming out of the closet? No, it was just an ordinary piece of thread.

Now, wait a minute. What was that? A piece of something, a bit thicker than string, light brown and hanging over the back of my aunt's chair. As I looked at it, it twitched and bobbed back and forth, like a wagging tongue. That must be it! I pounced and pulled for all I was worth. And pulled, and pulled; it kept coming.

"Chi Chi!" My aunt stood up from her chair and glared at me. I'd unravelled half of the sweater she was knitting! Boy, was I in trouble.

I was sent straight back to bed, and the grown-ups forced me to promise that I wouldn't pull any more hanging threads. So I resigned myself to a sleepless night, sitting up watching the baby while I tried to come up with a better plan for the next Friday.

I thought hard all week. After a while, I realized that while I'd promised not to pull any threads, I hadn't said anything about *cutting* them! I went through the sewing kit and found the best pair of scissors; I kept them hidden in my pockets at all times.

When Friday came, I was good and ready. But nothing happened. Nothing even remotely like a tongue came sneaking into our room; there were no suspicious threads to be found, anywhere.

Another week, and another Friday. Still nothing. I began to feel more relaxed, until I suddenly realized what the manananggal was up to. My baby sister was getting chubbier every day, and I was sure that the creature was just waiting for her to get more appetizing.

I had to be more vigilant. I began inspecting every stranger who came to my grandfather's store, to see if anyone was taking an unusual interest in the baby. That Friday, a pretty young woman came in. She played with my baby sister, smiling and cooing at her. A manananggal for sure!

I glared at her so fiercely that she stepped back, startled, with a strange look on her face. Ha! She knows I'm on to her plan, I thought. As she left, I felt certain that she'd be back that night because the moon was full.

This time I decided that I would search everywhere in and around the house, looking for the monster's tongue, her lower body, her winged upper half, whatever I could find. Meanwhile, the baby was with my nanny, while everybody sat around out front telling stories.

First the bedroom. Nothing. In the bathroom I saw a few threads, but they were just from an old towel. I cut them anyway, figuring I needed practice with the scissors. Moving on through the foyer — empty — I wandered out to the back porch.

That's when I saw it: a thin piece of silvery string, translucent, not at all like any thread I'd ever seen before. It was stretched taut across the back porch, pieces of its length gleaming in the moonlight filtering through the branches of the mango tree. I followed it and saw that the other end must be in the kitchen — where I had left my sister!

There was no time to call for help. The creature could be stealing my sister's life already! I felt my heart hammering, but I knew what I had to do. I pulled out the scissors and tried to cut the glistening tongue, but they wouldn't go through! I tried harder, pulling on the tongue as I sawed away, using the scissors like a knife.

Eeeekk! Creeek! There was a screeching sound, like grating metal. I knew I must be hurting the manananggal, to make her cry out in pain like that. Try to steal my sister's life, will you? Take that! I kept pulling and cutting and the screeching grew louder.

Finally, wham! The tongue was severed, and it whipped out of my hand, retreating back into the darkness. There was a loud thud out in the gloom of the backyard. I was elated. Chi Chi the hero!

The noise brought everyone running. "What was that? Chi Chi, are you all right? What's going on?"

I saw my sister, snug in my mother's arms, and I gathered the baby up for a big hug. I started to tell the story of my glorious victory, of how I had saved this poor innocent child from the powers of darkness ... And then I saw my mother staring out into the yard. From the expression on her face, I could tell I was in trouble again.

I had cut the brand-new plastic clothesline. The line had slipped off its squeaky metal wheels, and the day's laundry was scattered all over the muddy yard!

Moans and Groans

Chris Lindgren

Laura and Chris were sisters. Laura was the older sister and Chris was the younger. As the older sister, Laura naturally knew everything there was to know about everything. She told many fantastic tales to her little sister. Chris believed every last one of them.

One day, while they were both playing in the basement, Chris heard a strange squeak behind the furnace.

"What's that noise?" she asked.

"Oh that ..." Laura replied slowly. "I wasn't going to tell you anything about that. You would just get scared."

"What is it? You have to tell me!" demanded Chris.

"There are ghosts down here," Laura whispered.

"No way! Mom said there aren't such things as ghosts!"

"That's because Mom still feels guilty about what happened," explained Laura. "A long time ago, before you were born, a little boy and a little girl went for a walk in our basement. They got lost and were never seen again. Maybe they drowned in the septic tank or starved to death finding their way out of the junk room. They were never heard from again. Now their ghosts are still trying to find their way back home."

"I don't believe you." Chris was not convinced.

"It's true! Have you ever noticed how, when we go to visit someone's house, Mom always says, 'Don't go snooping around in the basement'? It's because she's scared the same thing will happen to us!"

"You're right! She does say that ... It must be true then. There are ghosts down here! What are we going to do? Wait a minute. How come you're not scared of these ghosts?"

"Oh," said Laura, "I know the magic words."

"You do? Well, then you have to teach them to me, too!" insisted Chris.

"All right. I'll let you in on the secret just this once. The words are easy:

"Moans and groans they don't scare me,
Moans and groans they don't scare me.

"You have to slap your knees in time when you say the words, like so —" And Laura repeated the words with Chris while they both slapped their knees in time to the magic words.

"Moans and groans they don't scare me,
Moans and groans they don't scare me."

After that, Chris felt safe from ghosts whenever she had to go into the dark, creepy corners of the basement or anywhere else in the house. She felt quite safe, that is, until a few days later, when she was getting ready for bed.

"I wouldn't walk too close to your bed at night if I were you, especially with your bare feet showing," warned Laura.

"Why not?" asked Chris.

"Because the green hairy monster lives under the bed. He's especially fond of dirty feet with toe jam. If he smells your little bare feet, he'll pull you under, and all that will be left of you will be the burp when he's finished."

"I don't believe you!" replied Chris. But just to be sure, Chris checked under her bed. Sure enough. It was dark under there, just the sort of place for an unspeakable green hairy monster to lurk. She was sure she saw an eye blink ...

Chris was smart, though. Instead of walking by her bed, she ran. She began in the kitchen, ran through the living room, down the hallway, sailed past the door and landed SMACK on her bed.

Chris's mother appeared at the bedroom door. "How many times have I told you never to jump on your bed! You'll break the springs! Don't let me ever catch you doing that again!"

When her mother's footsteps faded down the hall, Chris wailed, "Oh what am I going to do now? If I walk past my bed, I'll get eaten by the green hairy monster. If I jump on my bed, I'll get heck from Mom. I don't know which is worse."

Laura seemed unconcerned, however, and when Chris looked over at her big sister, she noticed that Laura's feet were dangling over the edge of the bed as she read her comics.

"Wait a minute. How come you're not scared of the green hairy monster?"

"Oh," replied Laura, "I know the magic words."

"You do? Well, then, you have to teach them to me, too," demanded Chris.

"All right," said Laura. "The magic words begin just like the ones for ghosts, only we add a line:

"Moans and groans they don't scare me,
I'm as tough as tough can be.

"When you say the last line, you wave your fist to show the green hairy monster how tough you are."

Together Laura and Chris chanted their magic spell, slapping knees and waving fists in the air.

Chris was safe in all the dark corners of her house once more. She knew the magic words. But a few days later, when they were both in bed, Laura turned to her little sister and said, "Guess what Sharon and I saw after school today?"

"I don't know. What?" replied Chris.

"We saw a bat. In broad daylight."

"So?" asked Chris.

"Well, everybody knows that bats only fly at night. So a bat flying in the day must be a vampire at night."

"What's a vampire?" asked Chris.

"My dear little sister! Don't you know anything? A vampire is one of those ghastly looking guys with white skin, slicked-back black hair, a long black cape, and sharp fangs for teeth. They come up to your bedroom window, push it open, creep up to your bed, bite you on the neck and suck out —"

"I don't want to hear any more about it! That sounds horrible!" interrupted Chris.

"And there's one right here in our neighbourhood!"

"Oh no!" Chris was overcome with terror until she suddenly realized something. "Hey, wait a minute. You sleep right beside me in this room. How come you're not scared of the vampire?

"Oh," said Laura, "I know the magic words!"

"You do? Well, then, you will have to teach them to me, too."

"Oh all right," agreed Laura. "The magic words begin like the others:

"Moans and groans they don't scare me.
I'm as tough as tough can be.
Cross my heart, I hope you die!"

Laura crossed her arms against her chest on the last line for extra protection.

"It doesn't rhyme," observed Chris. "I thought all magic spells had to rhyme."

"That doesn't matter," replied Laura. "It works for me. After all, I've never been bitten by a vampire."

That was certainly true. Chris repeated the magic words with her sister:

"Moans and groans they don't scare me.
I'm as tough as tough can be.
Cross my heart, I hope you die!"

It worked, too. The vampire left them alone that night.

Chris was indeed perfectly safe until a few days later. The two sisters were playing in the back yard when Laura brought up an important matter.

"You know why we haven't seen the neighbour's cat lately?"

"No. Why?" asked Chris.

Laura took a deep breath. "You know that new lady who just moved in down the street, the one with the long black hair, who wears sunglasses even at night, and drives that green car?"

"Uh huh …"

"She's a witch!" hissed Laura.

"Oh no!" Chris shuddered.

"Oh yes! Robert said he saw her grab that cat by the tail. She dragged it into her garage, skinned it alive, and then she threw it into her witch's brew!"

"No!' gasped Chris.

"Oh yes!" Laura continued. "And you better watch it on your way to school tomorrow. You'll have to walk right by her house. Maybe her next recipe will call for one plump little girl."

"Oh no!" wailed Chris. But then something dawned on her. "Wait a minute. You're a girl too, and you have to walk past her house on the way to the same school as me. How come you're not scared of the witch?"

"Oh," said Laura, "I know the magic words."

"You do? Well, then, you have to teach them to me, too," insisted Chris.

"Oh all right," Laura agreed. "But this is the last time I'll save you. The spell begins like the others:

"Moans and groans they don't scare me.
I'm as tough as tough can be.
Cross my heart, I hope you die.
Leapin' lizards fly by-by!"

Laura leaped into the air and flapped her arms wildly on the last line.

Chris repeated the words until she knew them thoroughly.

The next day Chris walked down the road on her way to school. As she walked past the witch's house, she saw a face looking out the window.

"Uh oh," thought Chris. "She's giving me the Evil Eye! But I'll show her! I know the magic words!" With shaking hands, she put down her lunch and her books, boldly faced the witch's house and said:

"Moans and groans they don't scare me.
I'm as tough as tough can be.
Cross my heart, I hope you die.
Leapin' lizards, fly by-by."

Then she picked up her books and went merrily on to school.

About half a block behind walked Laura and all her friends. They couldn't hear what Chris was saying, but they saw her slapping her thighs, shaking her fist, crossing her heart, and flapping her arms while leaping up and down.

"What's gotten into your little sister, Laura?" they all asked.

Laura turned all red, and then groaned. "I told you my little sister is crazy! This proves it. She flaps about the house like that all the time. It's so embarrassing!"

Chris had no idea what Laura was saying about her. She felt great. In fact, she felt tough as tough could be.

Late that night Laura and Chris were asleep. Mom and Dad were asleep. The goldfish were asleep. All was quiet. There were no ghosts, no vampires, no green hairy monsters or witches in the house. However, there just happened to be a very ordinary burglar in the neighbourhood.

He tried the front door. It was locked. He tried the back door. It was locked, too. He tried the basement window. It was not locked. He crawled inside, crept up the stairs and looked around for something valuable to steal. He loaded up his big sack with jewellery, silverware, some antique ornaments, the grocery money, a boom box and a Troll doll that he could hold for ransom.

Now just at that moment, Chris woke up. She was thirsty and wanted a drink of water. Very quietly she tiptoed down the hallway. As she passed the living room, she heard something. Looking up, she was horrified to see a large figure moving around in the darkness. She wasn't sure if it was a ghost or a vampire, but that didn't matter, because she knew the magic words! At the top of her lungs, she bellowed:

"Moans and groans they don't scare me.
I'm as tough as tough can be.
Cross my heart, I hope you die.
Leapin' Lizards fly by-by!"

The burglar spun around and saw a ghost-like figure flapping around in a long white robe. "It's a witch! It's a ghost! It's the *green hairy monster*!" he cried, and, dropping his loot, he ran through the front door without even bothering to open it.

Chris's mother and father heard the commotion and rushed out to see what was happening. When they found out that their little daughter had scared away a real live burglar, they were amazed. They were so proud of her, they told Laura all about it at breakfast the next morning.

After that, Laura was very careful about what stories she told to her little sister. After all, Chris had an even bigger story to tell, the same one I've just told to you.

Shhh ...

Da Trang

Tony Montague

Long ago and far away, deep in the rainforest of Vietnam, there lived a hunter whose name was Da Trang. Every morning Da Trang took his bow and his quiver of arrows and followed the same trail to go hunting. One day, as he passed beside a great banyan tree, he was distracted by a bird up in the branches and came within a footfall of stepping on, not one, but two bright green and highly venomous snakes! They were twined around each other. With lightning reflexes, Da Trang drew his bow to shoot.

But he did not shoot. He just stared at the two snakes, and the snakes stared back, unblinking, unmoving. And the longer Da Trang gazed down at the deadly creatures, the more his fear gave way to fascination. He was overwhelmed by the intensity of their colour, the intricacy of their markings, the brilliance of their sheen, and the grace of their movements, as slowly the two snakes began to uncoil from each other. For what seemed a long time, Da Trang stayed transfixed by their beauty; at last he took a step backwards, walked around them and continued on his way.

The next day, as he passed beside the banyan tree, there were the two snakes once again. And once again Da Trang stood, mesmerized by their extraordinary elegance and beauty. Now every day, as Da Trang followed the trail through the forest to go hunting, he stopped to admire the emerald-green snakes that had come to live beneath the tree. Not only was Da Trang no longer afraid of them, he admired them, he respected them, he even began leaving offerings of food for them. Da Trang took these serpents as his allies.

One day, many weeks later, as he approached the banyan, Da Trang heard the sound of a furious struggle and saw a huge cobra attacking the two green snakes! At once Da Trang drew his bow and fired. The arrow cut through the cobra's hooded neck and it slithered off into the forest, pursued by one of the green snakes.

But its companion lay dead on the ground. Da Trang picked up the beautiful, smooth-skinned creature, now drooping lifeless from his hands, and tears welled in his eyes. He, the hunter who had always feared and hated snakes, was crying for one now. Da Trang buried the emerald snake beneath the banyan tree and placed forest flowers on its grave. Then he went home to his cabin, greatly saddened. He had lost his two allies. One was dead, and the other had fled.

That night Da Trang had the strangest of dreams. He dreamed that the surviving green snake came up to his cabin, into his cabin, up onto his bed, came sliding up to where his head lay upon his pillow. With its little forked tongue it licked Da Trang's ear, and whispered to him:

"Thank you, hunter, thank you for all the kindness you have shown to me and to my dead companion. And for your kindness I have a gift."

From its mouth the snake produced a silvery pink and grey pearl; and, with flickering tongue, it carefully placed the little object beside Da Trang's head.

"Next morning, before you go hunting, put this pearl in your mouth and keep it beneath your tongue. Guard it carefully and tell no one. Thank you, thank you for your kindness."

Then the bright green snake was gone.

At dawn, when Da Trang awoke, he could remember every detail of the dream. As he lay thinking about the snake's mysterious words and its gift, he noticed something on the pillow beside him. It was a little shimmering pearl! The snake had told Da Trang to put it in his mouth before going hunting, and to keep it beneath his tongue — so he did.

The first animal that Da Trang chanced upon that day was a wild pig. But his arrow missed, and the pig ran off to hide. As Da Trang was stalking through the underbrush, he passed beneath a tree. Perched on a branch above him were two crows. They were talking to each other in their language, and Da Trang could understand every word that they said!

"Kraar! No way. His eyesight isn't any good — not like a bird's."

"But his hearing is pretty good these days," Da Trang called out. Not only could he understand the two birds, he could speak to them as well! Such was the magic of the pearl beneath his tongue.

The crows nearly fell off their branch.

"Kraar rwakh! He's talking to us in our language!"

"Yes," replied Da Trang, "yes, I can speak your language — and if one of you will show me where the pig is hiding ...

"Then what? Then what?" croaked one of the crows eagerly.

"Then after I shoot and kill it, I will leave you the parts that I do not want."

So the crow led Da Trang to where the pig had gone to ground. This time the hunter's arrow did not miss the mark. Da Trang slit open the pig's belly, drew out the entrails, and left them on the ground for the crow.

"Gnaak! Kaa! Kaa! This is good, this is very good!"

"Yes, it is good. And I propose that from this time forth we should hunt together. You lead me to the game, and I'll leave you all the parts for which I have no use. What do you say?"

"Kai! Kai! I say yes!"

Thus it was that Da Trang became the most successful and the most famous hunter in all of Vietnam — thanks to the snake's magic pearl that enabled gave him to understand and to speak the language, not just of crows and other birds, but of all creatures. And of course he never revealed to anyone the source of his extraordinary powers.

But one day, after Da Trang had shot and killed a wild pig and left the entrails as usual for the crow, another bird came along and stole them. When the crow arrived, there was not a trace.

"Kraaa! Kraagh! That hunter! He's cheated me! I always knew he would!"

The angry bird flew off to find Da Trang.

"Kragh! Graak! What about my share of the hunt?"

"I left it on the ground for you — as I always do."

"No! There was nothing. You cheated me!"

"That's not true."

"You're a cheat — and a liar."

"Hey!" said Da Trang becoming angry in turn. "Don't ever call me that."

"Gnaak! Liar! Liar! Liar!"

Da Trang reached for his bow and, pulling an arrow from his quiver, he fired at the crow ... but missed.

The crow seized the spent arrow in its claws and flew off, croaking furiously.

"Kaagh! Kaagh! You'll pay for that! You'll pay dearly for that!"

The next morning, in the river that flowed through the capital of Vietnam, beside the king's palace, a corpse was discovered — with Da Trang's arrow stuck through it! Soldiers came and pulled the body from the river, and pulled the arrow from the body. Such was Da Trang's fame that they knew at once it was his arrow. So Da Trang was arrested, taken to the city and thrown in jail, accused of murder. No one would believe his protestations of innocence, and how could he explain? Even he did not understand ... the crow ... some black magic ... the arrow ...

As he sat in his tiny prison cell, staring gloomily at the wall, Da Trang noticed a column of ants climbing in great haste. Now Da Trang could speak the language of all the animals — the smallest as well as the largest — so he called out to the leading ant:

"What's all the hurry?"

The ant stopped and replied, "A flood. There's a big flood coming. Do as we do — head for the hills!" and it pressed on.

Da Trang shouted to the jailer, "Guard! Guard! Take me to the king, I beg of you! I have news, urgent news! It's a matter of life or death."

So Da Trang was brought before the king of Vietnam. On his knees he pleaded: "Your majesty, do not ask me how I know what I know, but believe me. The river is about to rise and burst its banks. The whole city will be under water, and many, many of your people will drown — unless everyone leaves at once for higher ground."

The king considered a long time. At last he spoke: "Prisoner, I don't know whether to trust you or not. But I cannot risk the lives of my subjects. So we will leave. However, if this turns out to be some desperate last-minute ploy by which you think to save your skin, you will die tomorrow, at dawn."

But it was true. No sooner had the king gathered all his people and left for the surrounding hills than the river rose up and burst its banks, and floodwaters submerged the entire city. Many thousands would have died, but, thanks to Da Trang, no one drowned. The king was deeply grateful to him.

"Not only do I release you from prison and believe your story about the crow and its wicked ways, but you clearly have extraordinary abilities. I need them in the service of my kingdom, and I hereby name you, Da Trang, my chief counsellor."

So it was that Da Trang the hunter became the most powerful man in all of Vietnam, besides the king, of course. And so it was that Vietnam became a very strong and very rich country. For Da Trang knew things no one else could possibly know. He knew when enemy armies had invaded the kingdom, he knew where they were, he knew how many they were — because the birds told him, the insects told him, the horses told him, the snakes told him. He knew when the floods and the storms were coming. He even knew when the earthquakes were coming. The animals know these things before we do and they told him everything. And Da Trang never once revealed the source of his powers — the shimmering pearl that he kept day and night beneath his tongue.

But one day the king had to visit one of the islands off the coast of Vietnam. As always the chief counsellor travelled at the king's side. It was the first time that Da Trang had been to the seashore.

He was amazed by all the strange and wonderful creatures that he found there and that — when the king wasn't looking, of course — he conversed with.

While Da Trang and the king were being rowed out over the shallow waters to board the royal ship, Da Trang heard the strangest of voices beneath the waves. He peered down and saw a family of squids. The adult squids were singing lullabies to the baby squids!

It was so weird and so wonderful — so bizarre, so beautiful — that Da Trang began to laugh, to laugh uncontrollably. He couldn't help himself. He threw back his head and the pearl fell out of his mouth and into the sea!

Appalled, Da Trang leaped from the boat into the shallows and began desperately churning the waters. "Your majesty! Bring soldiers! All your men! Please! They must help me."

"But what is it you have lost?" asked the astonished king.

"A pearl, a little pearl. It's very valuable. You can't know how valuable it is!"

Dozens of men waded out into the shallows and churned the waters with Da Trang in search of the pearl — but they found nothing. Da Trang waited until it was low tide and he wandered all over, plunging his hands down into the sand and sifting the grains through his desperate fingers. But he found nothing.

The following day Da Trang continued his search. But he found nothing. He searched every day for a week, every week for a month, every month for a year, for two, for ten, for twenty years. But he found nothing. Da Trang stayed by the seashore for the rest of his life, searching. He never gave up hope, but he never found the pearl again.

Buddhists believe that after we die we may be reborn on earth — although not necessarily as human beings; more often and more likely we return as animals. And the Vietnamese say that the restless spirit of Da Trang did indeed return, and is to be found to this day in those little crabs that live on the seashore between high and low tide and that we in the West call "hermit crabs."

In Vietnam they are called "Da Trang crabs," because the people believe that in these tiny creatures is the spirit of the hunter. With their one huge pincer they seem to be digging, but they're not digging, they're searching, searching among the hundreds, the thousands, the hundreds of thousands, the millions, the billions, the trillions of grains of sand for the pearl, the pearl that Da Trang lost, the pearl that the snake had given him, the pearl that once had given him the power to understand and to speak the language of all the animals.

The Two Tom Cats

Stanley Sparkes

One night, when the squids were in, we boys were down on the beach with a fire; I'd say, oh, maybe there were eight or ten of us there altogether. We had the fire piled high with driftwood to make big flames. Big flames were said to attract big squids.

I don't think that's right, because there were just as many big squids on parts of the beach that had no fire as where we were with the fire. In any case, the squids were in the thousands and we were in the water chucking them ashore. Such squirting! You never heard the like before in your life.

By and by I heard "Miaow!"

I looked around, and there on the beach was an old tom cat with a white spot on his chest. And behind him there were dozens of other cats — all the stray cats in Glovertown, I would say. Now I thought they were hungry, so I chucked some squids to them. "Miaow!" said the old tom cat. But he didn't eat the squid that was pitched near his mouth. As he came nearer I could see him more distinctly, because his eyes shone out like an owl's with a sort of greenish light. Then it looked as if he was coming to bite me or something, so I grabbed him and chucked him in the water. Then the other cats ran away.

Well, he came ashore and I chucked him in again. Eight times he came ashore, and each time I threw him back out again into the salt water. Each time he would say "Miaow!" On his ninth trip out into the water, he didn't head back toward the shore at all, but began to sink, as if he couldn't swim any more. I did feel a bit queer about that, I did.

Yes, we all stood there on the beach by the fire with the squids squirting out in the water and on land, and then that old tom cat reared up in the water on his hind legs, staring straight at me — yes, I swear it, he spoke to me — with a quavery voice, "Tell Tom Next-One that Tom Last-One is finished for good now," and then he just died there in the salt water.

When I got home that night, Father and Mother and our young tom cat were waiting up for me. I told them the story I have just told you.

"Look at young Tom, look at young Tom!" shouted Mother.

And well we might look, for young Tom was rearing up on his hind legs on the woodbox cover and swelling up with pride. At last young Tom shouted, "Great — old Tom Last-One is dead! Then I'm the Lord o' the Cats!" Then he rushed out through the door and was never more seen again.

The Gift of the Dream Teacher

Sheldon Oberman

There was a young man who wanted to know everything and right away. He talked to everyone he met and he learned a bit of this, a bit of that. Then he heard of an old man who knew so much that he could teach you whether you were awake or asleep.

The young man searched until he found where the old one lived. It was a small shack in a muddy village far away about five miles past Yehoopitz.

"What a dump!" he thought. "There's not even a door — just a piece of cloth." Still he called in, "Hey, in there! I hear you're pretty smart for an old man."

The Old One lifted the cloth and answered, "Sometimes I think I'm smart, but what do I know?"

"How about telling me something new?" the young man asked.

"I'm an old man. Everything I know is old."

"Look," said the young man, a bit on the edge. "I've got an hour, give me your best shot."

"An hour?" the Old One said. "That's a long time for someone with no patience. Come in." They entered a small, empty room. The Old One said, "Let's sit for that hour and think about what changes and what doesn't."

So they sat quietly on floor for twenty minutes, forty minutes, almost fifty-nine minutes. Finally the young man said, "This is a stupid waste of time."

"Fine!" said the Old One. "At least you've learned the way out."

So the young man stormed off, but as he pushed through the doorway he got tangled in the cloth. Suddenly, he was falling and he landed in a river that wasn't there before. He would have drowned, but the cloth kept him magically afloat even as the river swept him to the sea. He drifted for days until he was found by pirates. He joined their crew and wore the cloth as a pirate's sash as he sailed the seven seas. Finally he could no longer stand their wild ways and he escaped.

He landed on the shore of the desert and wandered till he met a tribe of nomads. He joined them, and his cloth became the long robe of a wanderer. He had many adventures. He even married a princess of the tribe. Together they ruled a desert kingdom, until at last they became very old. He spent his last years by an oasis, staring into the quiet water. He kept his cloth wrapped tightly around him to keep off the cool night breeze.

One day his grandson fell in the water and cried, "Help! I'm drowning!" He jumped in and saved the boy, but he himself sank down, down to the very bottom, and the darkness swallowed him.

It was then he saw faint light far away. As it came closer it looked like a glowing face smiling down on him, the face of the Old One that he'd met so long ago.

"You'll be fine. Don't you worry," the Old One said.

There he was — a young man again lying in the doorway of the shack. The Old One was untangling the cloth that was wrapped about him like a dry cocoon.

"What! What happened?" he sputtered. "I'm not old? I'm not in the desert? I — I —!"

"A dream," said the Old One. "I gave you a dream. In the last minute of the hour we shared together, you had a little dream."

"But I thought I lived a whole lifetime!" he said.

"Ah, yes," said the Old One. "That's how a life can be. You can rush along from here to there, learn a bit of this, a bit of that. But when that life is over, there you are — on your back sputtering, 'What? What happened?'"

The young man looked deeply into the Old One's eyes and asked, "Will you teach me real knowledge?"

"That takes real time and real work," said the teacher. "All I showed you was an illusion, empty magic to get your attention."

"I will stay and learn from you," said the young man, "as long as you will have me."

The Old One draped the cloth upon the young man's shoulders so it became his prayer shawl as the young man began to learn the Old One's way of knowledge.

The Ridge
Road

Dan Yashinsky

It was a perfect night to drive up the pass — clear, not too cold, plenty of stars. I'm not much of a camper, but sometimes I like to spend the night by myself in the mountains. I do my best thinking when I can walk and talk out loud, something I've learned is better done alone in the mountains at night. On a downtown sidewalk, people just think you're nuts.

I drove over the pass and turned right on the gravel road that ran along the top of the coastal mountain range. When the road looped to the western side of the ridge, I could see the lights of Santa Barbara far below, and, out on the Pacific Ocean, the lights of the oil rigs and passing tankers. There were no lights on the east side, which ran down to steep canyons, a long river valley, and the San Roque mountains beyond.

I planned to park the car and hike another mile or two before making camp. My goal was the Ruins, the foundation of a mansion some millionaire had built, back in the boom years, on an impossible perch of rock overlooking the eastern canyons. It had fallen to pieces decades ago, and now only rattlesnakes enjoyed its handsome stonework.

I came to a level patch and coasted to a stop. The moment I turned off the car, the silence rolled over me. Moonrise wasn't until much later, but the stars gave enough light to walk by. I took out my pack — I was carrying a sleeping bag, tarp, bottle of water, and an orange for breakfast — then started my trek. A hiker wouldn't call my pace hiking. More just ambling along, murmuring and muttering, singing, talking, testing my thoughts on the clear night air.

> *"All my friends, the meeting is over*
> *And surely we must part*
> *And if I never see you anymore*
> *I will love you in my heart."*

The old hymn seemed to want singing, and that's what I did, enjoying my solitary tramp along the ridge road.

> *"The Lord is landing on the sea*
> *The Lord is landing on the shore*
> *The Lord is landing on the sea*
> *And we will shout 'Forevermore!'"*

A deep breath, then back to my hymn with a real mountain bellow:

> *"All my brothers, the meeting is over*
> *And surely we must part —"*

All of a sudden I stopped. Two people were standing on the road just ahead. Knowing how the sound carried, I knew they'd heard everything I'd been hollering for the last twenty minutes. I hoped they didn't think I was the Raving Sasquatch of the High Hills out to terrify the mountain dwellers that night.

I glanced up as I drew near and saw that the man and woman were watching me. They were holding each other and looked as if they'd been crying. Just before I walked by, the man spoke.

"We need help. Can you please come to our house?"

"What's wrong?" I asked.

The woman answered, "It's our son. He is very … restless tonight. Your song would help him go to sleep. We would like him to hear your good song."

It was bad enough to run into people on one of my excursions. Did they have to be lunatics as well?

"Sorry," I said, "I'm just out camping tonight. I'm not really —"

"Please," she said, with real urgency in her voice. "There's not much time. Please come."

I didn't really understand why they couldn't sing their own lullabies, but something about their strange, sad request caught me.

"All right," I said. "I'll come with you as long as you don't live too far. I still have to find a decent campsite tonight."

"You're welcome to stay on our property," the man said. "There's a good place to camp with a superb view of the valley. But you'll have to wait until morning to see it, what with this fog."

The fog had come up from the valley, and it swirled around us as we walked down a well-paved driveway. Ahead, the lights of a house made a warm glow in the thick fog. As we approached I noticed an odd smell in the foggy air, something acrid and unpleasant. As we walked up to the front door, the couple became more and more agitated. The man opened the door, his hand trembling.

"Please go to our son," he said. "He's in the bedroom on the left. We'll wait here." The woman stayed next to him, peering in with a look of terrible longing and sorrow, but she didn't seem able to cross the threshold.

"Sing to him," she whispered. "Sing to my little boy."

I went in. Despite the late hour, the child was far from sleeping. He was sitting in a chair, looking out the window. By the starlight in the room, I could see he was maybe four years old. He glanced at me matter-of-factly and didn't seem to find it odd that his parents weren't there, or that they'd sent a stranger into his room.

"Your folks are outside," I said to the child. "I met them on the ridge road and they wanted me ..." All of a sudden I felt very foolish. I'd come up to the mountains to sort out my own troubles and now I was supposed to play baby-sitter for these strangers. I glanced up the hall and could see his parents still standing there, looking in. "Well, your parents wanted me to keep you company."

The fog was pressing up against the glass, and the bitter, smoky scent had grown stronger. Without turning away from the window, the little boy said, "It's coming. It's coming up to the house this time."

Hearing his strange talk, I wished his folks had come in. They shouldn't have left him alone in the house, even for the time it took them to find me. I had no desire to sing a song to anybody, especially this kid.

"Do you want me to call your parents?"

"No."

"What would you like?"

"A story."

For a long moment he kept looking out the window. Then he turned and looked at me. I saw he was a handsome child, not so solemn when he turned away from his vigil.

"Could you tell me a story about me?" he asked, with a half-smile.

"Sure," I answered, without the least idea of what to say. Then I thought: I don't know this boy, but I do know the mountains pretty well. So I began my — our — story:

"Once there was a little boy who lived on a high mountain. He loved living in a place where the hawks flew, where the eagles hunted, where the trail ran in and out of deep canyons. This little boy knew all the secret places of the mountain, places full of sage and thyme. At night he listened to the coyotes, and in the day he would find where the rattlesnakes liked to sleep ..." The story went on for awhile, without much plot but full of the things I loved about the mountains.

I'm not sure how long I murmured the bedtime tale, but after a while I noticed the boy had fallen asleep in his chair. I pulled a blanket over him and looked again out the window. It was sealed with thick fog. The smell of burning was so strong that on my way out I checked the kitchen to see if the stove was lit. Everything was okay.

At the threshold the man and woman were still waiting. They were holding each other and weeping.

"Your son's asleep," I said.

"Thank you," the man said to me. "Just around that outcrop is a nice patch of grass for camping."

I walked away, pack in hand. Just before I passed around the rock, I looked back. The people were gone, and the house lights had been turned off. I couldn't smell that strange odour any more. The higher reaches of fog had started to break up, and the ridge was startlingly clear in the starlight.

> *"All my children, the meeting is over*
> *And surely we must part*
> *And if I never see you any more*
> *I will love you in my heart."*

I rolled out the tarp and my sleeping bag and went to sleep. I woke at dawn and took my orange out of the pack. From my campsite I had, as the man promised, a fabulous view of the valley and the inland range. A bank of clouds stretched below me all the way across the valley, like a white-grey river in some ancient riverbed. I sat for nearly an hour watching the sun rise. The wind came up, and the cloud-river began to flow down the valley.

Before hiking back to my car I thought I'd go down to the house and see how the little boy was doing. I pulled my boots on and stepped around the outcrop of rock that hid the house from my campsite.

I stopped. There was no house there. I was looking at the Ruins. The driveway I'd walked on the night before was an overgrown trail. The fine looking house had simply vanished, and in its place were the familiar stone foundations I'd visited many times before. The house was gone, and the man and woman and little boy with it. I hiked down the ridge road to my car and drove home.

The Fortune-Teller

Marie Anne McLean

In September of 1941, my mother was a WAAF (Women's Auxiliary Air Force, Britain) and my father was in the Canadian Army when they met in the home of my mother's parents in a village just outside Glasgow, Scotland. Within a couple of months they were engaged, and the wedding was set to take place the following July.

One evening shortly before the wedding, my mother and a group of her WAAF friends went to visit a fortune-teller. They were young and light-hearted in spite of the dire conditions of their world. Some of them were still in their teens. They swore they didn't believe that odd sort of thing, but life was all too serious and they were looking for a lark.

Much of what the fortune-teller said was what the girls had predicted, and each emerged from her session with a happy smile.

My mother's turn came at last. After my mother was seated at the table in the inner room, the fortune-teller began to rock gently and croon. She was a little round woman with ruddy weathered cheeks, and her hair in a twisted topknot. Her eyelids fluttered, and then she looked at my mother and began her prophecies.

Again much of what she had to say was predictable. She said that my mother was promised to someone from far away. My mother had removed her engagement ring, but this was still a fairly sure prediction. The country was filled with Allied soldiers from all over the world. British girls were meeting and marrying men from far away every day.

"You are going to know sorrow," she said.

My mother blanched. When your country is at war and you have given your heart to a rifleman, you do not want to hear that you are to receive the gift of sorrow.

Then the little woman rocked forward and said, "He'll be all right. He'll be hurt, but he'll be all right." And then she shook her head as though there was something obscuring her vision.

"There's someone who's worried about you, someone 'on the other side.' He's been gone a long time but he's watching over you and he's worried. He has very blue eyes, and half his face does not seem to move. He says you are going to suffer, but you are not to be afraid. He knows you'll be all right."

My mother thought that the little fortune-teller was quite something as an actress. It was pleasantly shivery, but nothing to be concerned about. When she next went home to visit the family, she told the whole story to her mother, my grand-mother, Jean. My mother finished the tale with a flourish. She told of the man with blue eyes.

My grandma Jean sat down abruptly. Her face was very pale. "That was my father. He had Bell's palsy; in the years just before he died, the left side of his face did not move. He had eyes like mine."

My great-grandfather, Robert Roy MacGregor, died when my grandmother was a little girl. It was from him that she inherited her dramatic blue eyes, so intensely coloured that the edges of the irises were navy.

The wedding was in July of 1942.

As the little fortune-teller stated, my father was all right. He was seriously injured in the early hours of the D-Day landing, but healed and survived the fighting of the liberation winter in the Low Countries in 1944-45.

The Piper's Tale

Jim Strickland

I'll tell you the story of Willie Johnstone the Piper. Now, Willie Johnstone was a tinker-man and he made his living travelling this way and that way, making baskets from the willow, or carving clothes-pegs, or doing a bit of hawking; this and that, and he'd work for the farmers now and again. But the main way he made his living was playing the bagpipes.

Och, he was a grand piper, was Willie Johnstone! There wasn't a games or gathering the length and breadth of Scotland that Willie Johnstone wasn't winning the cups and medals. There wasn't a competition that he didn't come first in. He was known the length and breadth of the country as just about the best piper there was.

Willie was a married man. He was a young man and he had a young wife, Maggie was her name; and she was an Argyllshire woman. They had two children; oh, two bonny wee bairns they were, a boy and a girl. They were a happy family, happy as they could be. They didn't always eat well and they weren't always as warm as they might have been, because they lived in a wee tent most of the year, you see. And they travelled about Perthshire doing this and doing that, earning their living the best way they could.

Anyway, it was coming up for the salmon-fishing season, and all the gentry and all them with money would be going to the town of Pitlochry for salmon fishing. Oh, there are some good, good fishing waters around the town of Pitlochry. And they decided they'd go down to the town of Pitlochry, Willie to play his pipes around the houses and the hotels, and Maggie to do a bit of hawking, to sell the baskets and clothes-pegs and other things she made.

So they hitched up their little cart, they hitched up their little Highland shelty to the cart, and they took it away up the back road, round up the back of Pitlochry. They got to the top of the hill yonder, and they put up their wee bow-tent, and Maggie made a fire and a little pot of stew for the children, you see, and they put the children down to sleep, and away they went, down into the town of Pitlochry.

They got down there, and Maggie went her way with her baskets and her clothes-pegs; and away Willie went to the hotels where all the gentry would be staying. Och, he expected to make good money that night, for he was well known among the gentry; particularly those who were army men, you see. Oh, they could tell a good piper when they heard one.

Anyway, Maggie, she did good business, she did good business that night; she'd made a few pennies at the doors. There was always people willing to buy her baskets and her scrubbers. Away she went, back up again. It was getting late, and she went back up to the town of Pitlochry. And there was no sign, no sign at all of Willie Johnstone. "Och," she said, "he'll have made a shilling or two playing his pipes, and he'll be having a drink before coming back to sleep." So, away she went, up to the camp.

Now she was walking up the back road yonder, and she thought she'd like a smoke of her pipe, you see. So she sat down at the bank at the side of the road and she put her hand into the big pocket in the back of her apron, and she pulled out her pipe and pulled out her bit of tobacco, and she filled her pipe. She was looking around inside her big pocket to see if she could find some matches. But she didn't have a match; she couldn't find a match there at all. And she happened to look around behind her into the field, you see. There on this little knoll in the middle of the field was this little cottage.

Now, it was it was a cottage in the Highland manner, a little black house in the Highland manner, not common around there at all. "I don't remember seeing that on my way down," she said. "Oh well, I wasn't in mind to be thinking about things like that." So she decided to go and ask for a light for her pipe, you see.

Away she went, and she knocked on the door. The door opened, and there was an old hag of a woman, with her hair hanging in rat-tails and not a tooth in her mouth but a few blackened stumps, and every crack and crinkle in her face was filled with the dirt of ages. "Och, what do you want here?" said the old woman.

"Oh, I'm just a poor tinker-body; I would like just a light for my pipe, a wee brand from your fire to light my pipe."

"I suppose I can give you that," she said. And Maggie went in and took a little branch from the fire and lit her pipe, and away she went up to the camp.

There was still no sign of Willie Johnstone.

"Oh, he's got himself in trouble down there in Pitlochry," she said, "and he'll be spending a night in the cells again. I'll see about that in the morning." So she made some supper for the children, and put them down to sleep. The next morning, first thing, away she went down into the town of Pitlochry, and straight to the police station she went. "Have you got my Willie in there?" she said.

"Och, no Willie was here last night. He had a drink or two, but he didn't get into any trouble. We had no reason to lock him up last night."

So she asked here and she asked there, around the town. They'd all seen Willie last night, and they'd all listened to his piping, you see, and they'd had a few drams with him; but no, they didn't know where he was now. So she stayed there for two or three days, just waiting to see if Willie would come back. But, no, after two or three days, he hadn't come back.

Now it was getting on for time to go down to the potato harvest in the Lowlands. She'd better get down or she wouldn't get a job, you see. So she packed up the camp and loaded up the shelty, and away she went, down to the Lowlands, thinking that Willie would catch up with her. Well, Willie didn't catch up with her there either. Not for many a long year after that. Och, for twenty years or more she never saw Willie Johnstone, her husband.

By this time the children had grown up and they were away their own road. They had married and they were away their own road, and it was a poor old Maggie by this time, you see. Doing the best she could now — but folks wouldn't buy the baskets or the scrubbers or the clothes-pegs she'd made. They'd rather go down to the stores and buy something made of plastic, you see; it was much easier. It was a poor old Maggie, following her wee shelty around, trying to make her living the best she could.

And one day she found herself near the town of Pitlochry. Oh, the memories that that brought back! So she went up the back road of the town, up to the hill there, and she set up her camp. She tied up her little shelty and she put up her little bow-tent, and away she went, down into the town of Pitlochry. But things were as bad there as anywhere else. She didn't sell a thing. The only thing they would give her here were a few bones and scraps to feed herself. With those few scraps she walked by, up the road.

Now, she sat down on the bank by the side of the road, and she thought she's have a smoke of her pipe, you see. So she put her hand in the big pocket at the back of her apron and pulled out her wee pipe; and she pulled out her tobacco and she filled her pipe. But she looked around and, och, she didn't have a match on her! What would she do? The poor old soul couldn't have a smoke of her pipe.

Now she happened to glance around her into the field, and there in the middle of the field was this little knoll, and on that knoll was a little house. It was a little cottage in the Highland fashion, not common around that part of Scotland at all. "Now, I can't remember seeing that on my way down," she said, "but, och, I wasn't thinking about things like that at all." So she decided to go there and ask for a light for her pipe. She

knocked at the door and this old hag of a woman opened it —
and her hair was hanging there in rat's-tails, and there wasn't a
tooth in her mouth but a few blackened stumps, and the wrinkles
and cracks in her face were filled with the grime of an age.

"Och, get away, get away! I have no time for the likes of
you tonight," she said.

"Oh, just a light for my pipe, Missus, that's all I'm asking;
a light for my pipe for a poor old tinker-body."

"No! I have company tonight," she says, "and I have no
time for the likes of you. Go on, get away with you! Get away
with you!"

"For a poor old tinker-body like myself, a poor old soul
like myself, just a light for my pipe, that's all I'm asking."

"Och, well, I suppose I can give you that."

Now, Maggie was bending down at the fireplace to take a
little brand of burning wood to light the pipe. There was a
door at the other side of the room, you see; and it was open
just a crack, and the light was shining through it. And she
thought she heard the sound of bagpipes. She listened. It was
the sound of bagpipes. And, oh, she recognized that playing!
That was the playing of her man, Willie Johnstone!

She made a dash for that door and she threw it wide open.
And it wasn't a little Highland cottage at all. It was a big hall,
with chandeliers hanging, and tapestries on the wall; and all
these wee folk, inches-high they were. And they were dancing
and they were reeling and they were whooping! And there,
playing the music for them, was Willie Johnstone, her husband, himself no more than inches-tall.

She made a grab for him. She grabbed him by the arm and
she pulled him out of that place. Now the old woman, she

grabbed the other arm and was pulling him back, and they were pulling this way and that way and this way and that way; and for all the love she had in her for her man, she gave one great pull and pulled him right past the threshold-stone of the house!

The house disappeared.

There was Willie Johnstone, standing there, up to his full height. And not a day or a minute older was he than the last time she had seen him. She fell at his feet, crying, "Oh Willie! Oh Willie Johnstone, my man! Where have you been all these years?"

"Get away from me!" he said, and he lifted his foot and gave her a kick. "I have a wife and a family up at the top of the hill there, and I've got to get up to them!" And away he strode, off over the fields.

She lay there sobbing. Oh, she was breaking her heart! Then the realization came to her; he had been taken by the fairies. For they have no music of their own, you see, and they have to have human musicians to play for their dancing, for they're awful fond of their dancing. And among the fairies there is no time. And he wasn't a day or a minute older than the time they had taken him.

And that's the story of Willie Johnstone, the Piper.

The Man Who Had No Story

Michael Burns

There was a man around here in the olden times. He was from out there, near Spunkane. He'd be a cousin now of Din Galvin that died there before Christmas, and he was poorly off, God knows. He had the grass for nine or ten cows, but no stock to be putting on it, and the times were hard then, what with rack-renting landlords and the blight on the spuds.

And didn't he decide to try his luck and go out looking for work as a *spailpin fanach* — a travelling farm worker — at the hiring fair above in Macroom, in the county Cork. The big farmers above in the Golden Vale'd always be looking for workers. They'd need 'em, for the rich red land there was so fertile that the ground would be groaning with the weight of the crops on it. It was that rich that if a man put a scythe down to stop for a bite to eat, he wouldn't find it when he'd come back, for the grass would be after covering it.

Well, anyways, to make a long story short and a short story merry, he took the world for his pillow and the sky over it for his blanket and he hit the road for Cork. And one evening, with the night drawing down and a wee bit of drizzle falling, wasn't he glad when he clapped eyes on a small cottage up ahead and a light in the window and smoke in the chimney. So he followed on 'til he got landed up in front of the door. He knocked on the door, and the door was opened to him. An old man and an old woman were inside. And they brought him in and sat him down and gave him a good feed.

When he was finished with eating, the three of 'em sat around the fire. And the old woman asked him if he had any news of the big world, for at that time 'twas the travelling people that'd be radio and newspaper all rolled into one. "Devil a bit," he said, for he was a bit of a shy man. Well, wasn't he mortified altogether when the old man, between two pulls on the *dudeen* — clay pipe — asked him if he wouldn't relate a story for them to be shortening the night!

"I have no story," he said, "and I'm no good to entertain the people at all." That didn't go down well, I'm telling you, for at that time in Ireland and 'tis still the case, you'd be expected to sing a song or tell a story or play a tune, if you were given hospitality.

The old man took another couple of pulls on the pipe, and then he said to the *spailpin fanach*, says he, "Well, you could make yourself useful and go down to the well and draw up a bucket of water, to be having there for the morning."

"I will indeed," said the traveller, and he took the white enamel bucket and pushed out the door.

Well, he put the bucket on the hook above the well and he was letting it down nice and easy when he felt a pull on it. He thought the bucket was catching on the side of the well somehow. So he gave a bit of a pull on it. Begor, that was when he got the fright of his life, for there was the mother and father of a pull from the other end, so much so that he was pulled arse over elbow, head over heels, and he fell for what felt like three eternities 'til he finally ended up in a heap, in pure darkness. He was feeling himself to see if he had anything broken when he heard voices. And when he looked around, didn't he see three men with bog-dale splinters for light, and they carrying a coffin. Big, dirty, black-bearded blackguards of men, and they arguing among themselves.

"And who will be the fourth man to shoulder the coffin?"

"The *spailpin fanach*, wherever he is!" they shouted.

Well, the fright he got when he fell was nothing compared to the way the heart went sideways on him when he heard that.

"There he is!" said the three of 'em when they spied him. "Catch a hold of the coffin, and be giving us a hand."

What else could he do? He had no sooner settled in under the coffin than they were off, like March hares over hills and high places, through sloughs and swamps, bog-holes and furze bushes. And the poor *spailpin fanach* running like the devil, his clothes tearing on briars and brambles, and his feet soaking and dirty water running out of his boots, and the three big buckos giving him every dirty look if he fustered or faltered, looks that'd sour milk or peel paint from walls. Well, he was nearly half-dead with this midnight marathon when the mad race stopped.

And he looked up and nearly fell out of his stand. For where do you think they had fetched up but outside *Keelawarnogue* graveyard — the "graveyard of young men."

"And who'll pass the coffin up to us?" said the three buckos. "The *spailpin fanach*, of course."

Well, if he wasn't stuck with the job of trying to get the coffin up over the graveyard wall, and it all of eight or nine feet if it was an inch. In the heel of the hunt, by dint of hard pushing, if he didn't get the coffin up and over the wall. He was going to take his leave of the three boys. "Not so fast," says they. "Who'll dig the grave?" says they. "The *spailpin fanach*, of course."

So the poor devil was digging the grave, and hard, dirty work it was too. And the three lads watching every move, eyes on 'em like travelling rats. Until finally he had the grave dug and he scrambled out of it.

"And who'll go in the coffin?" said their leader. "Who else but the *spailpin fanach*!" says the other two.

Well, when he heard that, that beat all! As quick as you'd be pulling out your handkerchief to catch a sneeze, he started into running and the three boys after him with every curse darkening the air around him. He made a desperate dive for the graveyard wall, and if there was Olympic medals for clearing walls he had 'em all swept. And the three lads after him, swearing like sailors. He ran like a man possessed, a hill at a leap, a glen at a step, and thirty-two miles at a running jump until in the latter part of the night he could see no sign of *toir* — pursuit — and he went up to a house and pounded wildly on the door, so the people inside would give him protection.

When the door opened, who was it only the old man from the night before, a wicked gleam in his eye. "You'll not be short of a story now," he said. When the *spailpin fanach* heard this, he fell into a dead faint on the spot.

When he woke the next morning, where was he but beside a well, with a white enamel bucket beside him, full of water. He picked up the bucket and turned to bring it with him to the house. But where the night before there was a little thatched cottage, there was now nothing but ruins.

Well, I'll tell you this now and I'll tell you no lie, he didn't use much in the way of shoe-leather until he got as far as Farranfore village and away with him into the nearest public house, and 'twas a double whisky and two pints of porter before he could talk.

But d'you know this, that same man was never short of a story again as long as he lived. And the best story he had was the first story he got, even if it was dearly paid for.

If there's a lie in it, it wasn't me that composed it. I only have what I heard, I only heard what was said, and MOST of what was said was LIES!

Reaching
Across

Room for One More

Gail de Vos

My cousin Joseph was living alone on the top floor of a downtown high-rise apartment building when his friends invited him to spend the weekend at their newly renovated home in the country. He had never been there before but thought he could find it easily ... even in the dark.

His friends gave him directions, telling him that it was easy to find. "Joseph, there are only two houses on the road, but ours you just can't miss. It's an old white three-storey farm-house — huge — with a wide gravel driveway that completely circles the house. We'll leave the lights on for you."

His friends knew Joseph well. His most dependable trait was that he was late for everything — he always had a good excuse, but was always late. And this time was no exception. Although Joseph had written the directions down carefully, during the hectic time he had trying to leave his apartment, and then the city, he left them by the telephone.

He knew the general direction of the farmhouse and its approximate location, however. Joseph's other well-known trait was his stubbornness. "How many roads can there possibly be around this town?" he thought to himself. After spending hours on the dark country roads, Joseph finally found his friends' house, and it was just as they had described it. It was large and luminous white in the moonlight. In the brightness of the yard lights, he could easily see the circular gravel driveway.

Although by this time it was very late, Joseph drove up to the house and parked his car by the front door. His friends opened the door sleepily. They told him to park his car around the back and to make himself at home in the guest bedroom on the third floor. They were going back to bed and would show him their house in the morning.

Joseph made his way to the bedroom, and after exploring the room and looking out of the window which overlooked the driveway and the darkness beyond, he got ready for bed. It was late and he was certainly ready for a good sleep, but for some reason sleep just would not come. He lay there for a long time but finally decided to get something to read.

As he got out of bed he heard a noise outside the window, and looked out at the darkness. Although his friends had extinguished the outside lights, the moon gave just enough illumination for Joseph to see ... an old-fashioned mail coach drawn by four coal-black horses on the gravel driveway below. Joseph stared in bewilderment, and then in amazement, as he watched a tall man descend from the coach. The man was the most repulsive being Joseph had ever seen. Not only was he as thin as a skeleton, but he had a long jagged scar that travelled down his face from just below his right eye, across the corner of his mouth, and disappeared into the high collar on the left side of his neck. As Joseph stared at him, the man raised a long bony finger, pointed straight at Joseph in the window and rasped, "There's room for one more."

Joseph pulled himself back from the window in horror. When he collected himself, he looked out again, but there was nothing there to see. No coach. No horses. And, no coachman.

"It's just a dream," Joseph thought to himself. "Or someone with a twisted sense of humour. But, just in case, I'll check the driveway in the morning. If it was truly a dream, there will be no signs of wheels and horses." Needless to say, Joseph could not fall asleep for the rest of the night. As the sun rose, he quietly made his way outside. The gravel showed no signs of horses and coach wheels.

"Just as I thought. It was a dream."

Still Joseph, disquieted from such a vivid experience, did not mention it to his friends. Instead he pushed it to the back of his mind and enjoyed the day. That evening, however, it happened again. He could not sleep. He heard the noise outside his window and he went to it. The same coach, the same horses and the same coachman were on the driveway below. He even heard the same warning! With his long finger pointing directly at Joseph in the upstairs window, the coachman repeated, "There's room for one more."

This time Joseph did not leave the window, but the coach and the horses and the coachman disappeared. They did not go anywhere; they just vanished from sight. "Enough," thought Joseph. He threw his belongings into his case, quietly but quickly went down the stairs and got into his car. He drove directly to his apartment, went upstairs and fell asleep without any more conscious thought.

Joseph slept well and long. When he arose, it was mid-afternoon. His immediate hunger drove all thoughts of his adventure from his mind. "I need to eat something and, of course, there's no food here." He decided to go to his favourite eatery a few blocks away. As he waited for the elevator, he began to register the long passage of time. A Sunday afternoon was not usually a busy time of day in his apartment building. What was taking so long? He was so hungry!

When the elevator finally arrived, Joseph saw how packed it was. There was just enough space for him to squeeze in. As he began to step into the elevator, however, a long bony finger pointed at him. The words calling out to him propelled Joseph to follow the voice to gaze at the revolting face of the coach driver.

"There's room for one more," he dimly heard echoing through his mind.

Without any thought at all, Joseph quickly hurled himself back out of the elevator and stood there trembling as the doors closed in front of him and the elevator car proceeded to descend. Joseph stood there, silent and not moving for a long time, then started to quiver and shake. But it was not him vibrating, it was the building! The cables on the elevator car snapped, the car fell to the basement and everyone aboard was killed.

Joseph never stayed in his apartment again and has since moved to a walk-up not too far from me.

The Bus to Winnipeg

Ted Stone

Michael didn't want to move to Winnipeg with his mother and brother. He wanted to stay in Sault Ste. Marie with his friends, where he could keep playing on his own hockey team, where he had lived all twelve years of his life.

"At least I get to sit by myself," Michael thought as he took his seat on the bus to Winnipeg. The bus was nearly full, and there weren't three empty seats together. His mother had therefore allowed him to sit alone. He chose one of the two vacant seats at the very back, across the aisle from the bathroom. His mother and younger brother, Andy, sat near the front.

Before the bus had pulled away from the station in Sault Ste. Marie, he could hear his mother scolding Andy for picking his nose. Michael didn't know who was more embarrassing, his nagging mother or snot-nosed little brother. As the bus manoeuvred through the narrow downtown streets Michael stared through his window at the snowbanks piled higher than the cars. He wondered if the snow banks were as high in Winnipeg.

Soon, the bus left the town, speeding along the highway going north and west around Lake Superior. The fading evening light turned into darkness, and the view from Michael's window became a reflection of himself. Sometimes, the bus passed by houses next to the highway. Occasionally, it passed, without stopping, through tiny villages. A flash of lights would whiz through the image on the window, and Michael would strain unsuccessfully to see beyond it.

Three times the bus stopped in small northern towns along the lake. Other passengers got off to stretch their legs and eat hamburgers and potato chips. Twice Michael's mother and brother got off, too. But Michael stayed on the bus. He knew his mother wouldn't buy anything to eat. She was saving money. She had a lunch packed that was supposed to last them through the night until the next morning, when they would get to their new home.

When the bus stopped at Nipigon, only a few people got off. It was nearly midnight, and many of the passengers were sleeping in their seats. Michael could see his mother, but his brother was out of sight in the seat beside her.

Michael leaned his head against the window and looked at his reflection in the glass. He watched the people standing in the cold outside the bus. He watched their frosty breath floating in the icy air. He looked at the Christmas lights in the windows of the stores.

Michael was nearly asleep when the driver returned, and only felt the bus as it inched forward up the hill out of town, gradually regaining speed on the highway to Thunder Bay.

He didn't even notice when the other boy sat down beside him. But after a few minutes he realized someone was there. He opened his eyes. He couldn't see anyone's reflection beside his own in the window. Somehow, though, he knew someone was in the next seat.

"Hello," a boy in a red toque said when Michael turned. "I didn't think anyone was sitting here, so I sat down." He held out his hand. "My name's Kevin," he said.

The boys shook hands, and Michael told his new seatmate his name. The boy's hand was cold so Michael guessed he had just got on the bus. "I didn't see you before," he said. "You must have got on at that last town."

The boy shook his head "I've been on this bus all day," he said. "I've been in Toronto visiting my father. I'm going home to Winnipeg."

"I'm going to Winnipeg, too," said Michael. "Only it's not my home. Not yet anyway. We're moving. My dad got a new job. He's been in Winnipeg for a month. It took him this long to find us a new house."

"You're lucky. My dad got transferred to Toronto. Only he never did find us a house. My parents ended up getting a divorce instead. Now I go to Toronto to visit him on holidays and in the summer. My mom used to take me, but I've been back and forth so many times she says I can do it myself now. It's only a day and a night on the bus, you know."

"You go by yourself? How old are you?"

"Thirteen. How old are you?"

"Almost thirteen."

"I'm almost fourteen. You'll probably go by yourself next year, too. Only your dad lives in Winnipeg, so you won't have to."

"Maybe I'll go back to the Sault and visit some of my friends."

"Maybe. But you'll like Winnipeg. There's lots to do there. I'd just as soon stay home for my holidays. But my dad wants me in Toronto, so I have to go back and forth all the time. I was there for Christmas with my mom."

"It must be fun getting to ride the bus by yourself."

"It's all right. But I want to go home. Last time there was an accident."

"What happened?"

"I figured you would have heard about it. But look, it's snowing again."

Michael looked up to see snow pelting against the bus's windshield. The wipers swung back and forth, scraping ice and snow in both directions across the window. From the back of the dark bus it looked as if they were in outer space. The snow was a meteor shower flying past them as they sped along.

"How can the driver see?" Michael asked.

"I don't believe he can," said the boy. At that moment, the bus slowed. Michael saw lights ahead on the highway. At first, he only saw headlights and the steady blinking of a light from a police car. But then, as the bus passed the scene in the night, he saw that there had been an accident.

He turned to look out the rear window. A transport truck and a Greyhound bus were lying in the ditch at the side of the road. An ambulance and police car were parked at the edge of the highway. Michael watched until he couldn't see anything any more. When he turned around, the boy who had been with him had disappeared.

Michael looked along the darkened rows of seats, trying to see where the boy had gone. But he couldn't find him in the shadows of sleeping passengers. He turned to look back at the accident, but he could see only darkness. He leaned his forehead against the window. His entire bus ride seemed like a dream. His mother and brother. Winnipeg. Sault Ste. Marie. The boy in the red toque.

In a few minutes, the bus pulled into the station in Thunder Bay. The driver announced a thirty-minute rest-stop. Michael decided to get off and find the other boy. His mother stood up by her seat and waved to him.

"Michael," she said when he got closer, "we're going to go in and have a hot chocolate or something warm to drink. What do you think?"

An hour before, Michael would have found the idea of drinking a hot chocolate with his mother and little brother objectionable. Somehow, though, in the middle of the night in Thunder Bay, it seemed all right. He'd even invite the boy in the red toque to join them.

Michael didn't see the boy in the restaurant, though. And when he asked his mother about the wreck on the highway, she said she hadn't seen one. Michael couldn't believe she had missed it. When the waitress arrived with their hot chocolate, he asked her if she had heard about a bus accident close to town.

"You must mean the bus that collided with the transport truck," said the waitress. "It was in a snow storm."

"That's right," said Michael. "The truck and bus both ended up in the ditch."

"That was a bad accident," said the waitress. "Lots of

people were hurt. A boy from Winnipeg was killed. It happened three years ago, just about this time of year."

"Three years ago?" Michael said.

"That's right," said the waitress. "It'd be just about three years ago exactly. I was working the graveyard shift that night, too. The bus from Toronto was late, and then the police came in and told us what happened.

"I knew that little boy. I recognized his picture in the paper. I remember him because he came through here just before Christmas. He was on his way to Toronto to see his father, riding all that way by himself. I remember he was wearing a red toque."

Michael sat quietly, barely touching his cocoa, until it was time to leave. Back on the bus, he sat, awake, riding through the night. Riding toward Winnipeg. Watching his reflection in the window. Somewhere near the Manitoba border, just as the sun was coming up, he looked down and, for a moment, he thought he saw a crumpled red toque on the seat beside him.

The Loup-Garou Ghost

Louise McDiarmid

Albert Dumoulin was a very brave man. Everybody said so. There wasn't anything he was afraid of.

Albert had a neighbour, old Henri. Henri had borrowed five dollars from Albert, and he was in no hurry to pay it back. "I'll pay you back next week," he would say. Or "I'll pay you back at the end of the month." But next week came, the end of the month came, and he still didn't have any money for Albert. Oh, he had money for this, and money for that, money for tobacco, for a new harness, for a new hat for his wife, but did he have the five dollars to pay back Albert? Not a penny! Albert didn't say anything to Henri, but he muttered in his beard all right. And then, one night, just like that, Henri died — still owing Albert the five dollars.

Now, the people around there, they believed that if a person died with an unpaid debt, his soul could not rest. They believed that the spirit of that dead person would appear to the lender of the money and ask him to forgive the debt, to make a gift of the money.

So Albert could expect a visit from the ghost of his old neighbour, Henri. Was he nervous? Not a bit! He was curious, in fact, to see what the old man would look like as a ghost. Having now to beg for the money would serve Henri right for being so slow in repaying that five dollars.

Albert waited for Henri's ghost to come and beg. Night after night he waited, but Henri did not come. Albert was very annoyed. It seemed that Henri was as devil-may-care about his debts after he was dead as he was when he was alive!

After a while Albert gave up waiting for his neighbour's ghost, and life went on. It was time for haying, time for harvest; they killed the pig, ploughed the fields, cut wood for winter. Then Albert went with his team of horses to work in the lumber camp, drawing logs out of the bush.

He had only been there a week when he first saw the wolf. He caught just a glimpse of it as he came long the trail at dawn one morning. It was a big one, grey like a shadow, with strange, glowing eyes. He saw it again the next day, and the day after. He began seeing it more and more often. When he was working alone, he would feel he was being watched, and he would look up to see it standing among the trees, looking at him.

One day it appeared at the side of the trail just ahead of him. It stared at him steadily, with its head cocked to one side, for a full minute. Then it ran off into the bush. Strange thing, when he got to where the wolf had been, there were no tracks in the snow! What kind of wolf was this, whose feet left no mark? Most men, they would have been frightened, but not Albert. I told you he was a very brave man.

And yet there was something familiar about that wolf. The way it cocked its head when it looked at him made Albert think of his old neighbour, Henri, he of the unpaid five dollars. The more he thought about it, the more Albert suspected that the wolf *was* Henri, come back, not as an ordinary ghost, but as a *loup-garou!*

And he was right. The next evening, as he was making his way back to the shanty, the woods were growing darker and darker all around him, when he noticed the wolf trailing along behind his sled. His horses were frightened; they broke into a gallop. The wolf kept pace. Albert pulled back on the reins, and slowed the horses down to a walk. The wolf slowed down also. Albert turned to look at the wolf, and the wolf looked boldly back at him — with the eyes of old Henri.

"Albert," said the wolf in Henri's voice, "Albert, give me the five dollars." Not "Please give me the five dollars" or "I beg you, Albert, forgive me that debt of five dollars I owe you," but just "Give me the five dollars."

Albert was annoyed. "No," he said, "I won't give it to you."

"You must give it to me," said the wolf.

"I don't have to," answered Albert.

The wolf-that-was-Henri came closer. Its eyes were like two burning coals now, and there was a bluish flame coming out of its mouth.

"Albert, Albert," growled the wolf. "Forgive my debt or you will be sorry."

"You were not in any hurry to pay me when you were alive," said Albert. "Now you can just wait until I am ready to forgive your debt." And he touched his horses with the whip, turned his back on the wolf and drove off down the trail.

Back to the camp they went, the horses, the sled, Albert and the *loup-garou*. Albert put the horses in the stable. The *loup-garou* sat in the shadows and watched. Albert went into the shanty. Before he could shut the door, the *loup-garou* had followed him in. Like a big dog, it followed at his heels, and yet it appeared that no one else could see it. Albert scratched his head. Well, if that was the game Henri wanted to play, let him be. He didn't care. He ate his supper. He went to bed. The *loup-garou* sat on the end of his bunk, staring at him with Henri's own eyes.

Albert couldn't sleep. He closed his eyes, but every time he opened them to see if the wolf was still there, it was. Staring at him, its eyes glowing, its breath coming out in a blue flame. He glared at it. The wolf glared back. He pulled the blanket over his head, but he could feel the *loup-garou* there, looking at him. He didn't sleep well.

It was there in the morning when he got up, and at his heels when he went to hitch up the horses; it followed his sled into the bush. Albert got used to having the wolf around.

But then things started to go wrong. He almost got hit by a falling tree. His harness broke, and he had to sit up half the night, mending it. His sled tipped over and spilled a load of logs.

One morning he found his boots chewed up. He had to get a new pair from the boss. Five dollars they cost him. He knew who had done that, all right!

A few days later his horses got sick. He couldn't work with them for two days, so he lost two days' wages — plus the five dollars it cost him for the medicine to doctor them.

Albert had had enough. "All right," he said to the *loup-garou*-who-was-Henri's-ghost. "I guess you've waited long enough. I'm going to give you the five dollars now. I forgive your debt."

And Henri-who-was-the-*loup-garou*, do you know what he said, that old rascal? Not "Thank you, Albert" or "Blessings on you, old friend" or anything like that! No, he asked for more! "Albert," he said, "how about asking the priest to say a Mass for my soul? It costs only five dollars, a High Mass."

And do you know what? Albert paid the priest to say a Mass for the soul of old Henri. But he didn't pay for a High Mass, the most powerful, the one costing five dollars. No, he paid for a Low Mass, less powerful, costing only two dollars. Because, you see, a man who takes his time about paying his debts should have to take his time about getting into heaven, too.

The Dead Don't Pay

Helen Carmichael Porter

There once lived in Toronto a young boy named David White. He had just turned twelve and wanted a new bicycle, but his parents told him that, with four children and a preacher's salary, they couldn't afford it. He'd have to earn the money himself. Soon after this, David spied a beautiful, streamlined racer bike beside an ad in *The Globe and Mail* that said "Paper Carriers needed! *The Globe and Mail* offers this snazzy new ten-speed bike to the carrier who signs up the most new customers and keeps them for a year. Call for information."

It was the answer to David's prayer. He'd get his bike and save money as well. He phoned *The Globe* and was invited to an interview with some other kids down at *The Globe* office. A route manager told them that they'd have to get up very early in the morning to pick up their papers and start their delivery. Every paper had to be delivered before 6:30 A.M. He showed them how to fold the paper so that they could deliver

102

it more efficiently, and gave them each a permission form for their parents to sign. That night, when David asked his mother to sign it, she frowned.

"You'll have to wake up at five o'clock in the morning," she said. "You're too young to go out so early. A growing boy needs his sleep."

David thought for a moment about this. "What if I promise to go to bed early, like eight o'clock?" This was a big concession on his part, but he wanted the bike dreadfully. He'd been riding his big sister's old blue bike for years, and he wanted a boy's bike more than anything else in the world. Then his dad said he thought it would be a good experience for David, so his mother signed the permission, with the warning that he'd have to quit if his schoolwork slipped.

As soon as he was hired, David started introducing himself to the old customers and canvassing for new ones. *The Globe* gave him sixty subscribers for his route, but he knew he could sign up a lot more if he worked hard. Hadn't he sold the most apples on Scout's Day? Didn't he fill his UNICEF box at Hallowe'en? Besides, his father was a local minister, and some of the parish people would surely take *The Globe and Mail* to help him out. Every day after school he went canvassing up and down the streets of his neighbourhood. Many people subscribed to the rival *Star* and *Telegram* newspapers, but they still listened as the slim, freckle-faced boy eagerly described the virtues of *The Globe*: "It's a morning paper so you get the news of the day fresh and early. It give the best international coverage." Some neighbours signed up on the spot. The oldest regular customer on his route was Miss Beggs. She was rumoured to be ninety-eight years old, a former schoolteacher

who lived with her nephew, a bespectacled chartered account-
ant. When David went to their house to say he was their new
carrier, it was old Miss Beggs who came to the door. When
she saw it was David, she chuckled, "Well, I enjoy my daily
paper. It keeps me going. David, I'm pleased you'll be bringing
me my *Globe* from now on."

By the end of the week, David had signed up another fifty
people. "Remember, you'll have to deliver all those papers
yourself," his mother warned as he counted up his subscriptions. But David's jaw was set. He wasn't going to let anything
stop him from getting his new bike.

The next morning he started his route. He rose when it
was still black outside, 5:00 A.M., and dressed warmly. His
mother got up and made him eat porridge, cocoa, a boiled egg
and toast. "You need something in your stomach to fuel your
energy." She sat in her plaid dressing-gown watching him eat,
warning him about strangers who might ask him indoors.
David listened as he chewed and swallowed. He was anxious
to be on his way.

Bundled warmly, pulling his wagon after him, he hurried
off to the street corner where his papers were dropped by *The
Globe* truck. Quickly, he folded them one by one, as the man
had shown them, and piled them in his wagon. Hurrying from
one house to another, he threw the papers up on their
porches. Sometimes he missed, and the papers opened up and
fell down into the garden and David had to go and hunt in the
dark bushes for it. Some fell open and blew apart, and David
had to fly around the garden after the rebellious sheets and
sections. By the time he'd finished the route, it was seven
o'clock and he was exhausted. But he knew better than to tell

his mother that, so when she asked him how it went, he snapped his fingers. "It was easy!" Off he went to school, and only the vision of that red shiny bike with all its bells and whistles kept him from falling asleep in class.

Though it was always dark, almost like the middle of the night, when David did his route, he soon got used to it and cut his delivery time by half an hour. After two weeks he went to collect the money, and this he found harder than delivering the papers. Some people were never home, many didn't have change, or they complained that they didn't receive their paper on such-and-such a day and didn't want to pay for that one. David politely listened and returned as many as four times to some homes. Sometimes one of his older sisters went with him to keep him company while he collected his money.

Miss Beggs was nice to collect the money from. She was always at home, and usually had his money waiting in her shaky, frail hand. Her voice crackled with pleasure when she said, "Thank you, David. You know, I just live for my daily *Globe*. It starts my whole day right!" David would leave her home with his face glowing as he revisited some of the more difficult customers who rarely paid him on time.

After four months, David was advised by the route manager that he had signed up the most customers of any carrier in the city. He was now so excited he began drawing elaborate sketches of the bike in his notebook, shading in the specific details of tail-lights, gears, streamers. Even the collecting didn't distress him as much as it used to, although one drunk customer chased him away when he came collecting at his dinner hour.

One week a large black hearse appeared at the end of his street, and David later discovered that Miss Beggs had died. The subscription wasn't cancelled, however, so he continued delivering the paper to the house. Miss Beggs's nephew paid by envelope, but David never saw him. He missed his conversations with the old woman, and her enthusiasm for her daily paper.

A few days later he found some new subscriptions waiting with the papers at the drop-off corner. These had been registered at *The Globe* office and added to his route. David glanced at them under the lamplight: 1440 Yonge Street, 88 Balmoral Crescent. He started up and down the streets of his route, which always ended at Poplar Plains Road, near his house. As he came up to 1440 Yonge Street, he looked up, down and around for the address. There was nothing but a dark laneway that cut between a store and a restaurant. Could there be a house at the end of the laneway? He peered down it but could see nothing except for a large hulking shadow, perhaps a little house or a garage. Cautiously, he started down the lane, feeling his way in the dark, the rolled-up paper in his hand.

At last he came to a small stone building, and behind it tombstones and monuments. The graveyard stretched out behind St. Clair Avenue for almost a block. Was the new customer the gravedigger, he wondered? Suddenly a light went on in a nearby building and David could see the names engraved on some of the tombs. The name "Beggs" caught his eye and he walked closer to read the writing on the stone. "Josiah Beggs, 1826-1930," "His wife, Dorothea Chown Beggs, 1840-1924." Then he could see the name of his customer freshly etched: "Jessica Beggs, 1870-1956." David felt his skin grow cold and the hair rise on his back and neck. He couldn't move. Then he heard a familiar voice speak: "Give me my paper."

He dropped the paper and ran as fast as his legs would take him back to the sidewalk to his wagon. He remembered that Miss Beggs enjoyed her paper, but wasn't this going too far? Dazed and frightened, he walked through the rest of his route, wondering if he should tell his parents. But remembering what his mother had said about strangers, he didn't want to worry her, and he didn't tell kids at school because he thought they'd never believe him.

The next morning he scanned the route list to see if the address was still there. It was. He hurried through his route, wondering if the bicycle was really worth this kind of effort. By the time he reached the graveyard he decided it was. He cautiously walked down the lane to the gravedigger's stone house. The tall Beggs monument stood like a sentinel waiting in the darkness. He hesitated; watching, listening. At first there was nothing but silence. Then the familiar voice spoke, a tad thinner and hollower than in life: "I do love my paper!" He aimed it at the base of the monument and turned and bolted out the laneway.

Sweating, with tingles running up and down his spine, he finished his route and went home. As he came in the front door, his mother looked at him from her sewing and said, "Are you all right? You're very pale."

David turned away from her worried gaze, saying, "Oh, I'm fine, Mom."

"I worry about you when you're out there by yourself in the dark."

He shrugged and smiled. "There's nothing to worry about. I'm fine." As he pored over his math homework in his room, he thought about his graveyard customer. He'd always liked Miss Beggs, alive. What was wrong with her getting her paper when she was dead? But he felt uneasy, and couldn't get to sleep. Later that night, he and his father were both in the kitchen fixing themselves snacks, and he asked, "Dad, do you believe in ghosts? I know you do a lot of funerals and see a lot of dead people. I just wondered."

His father spread some raspberry jam on toast as he answered. "Yes, I had three funerals last week, and I've got another tomorrow. Ghosts. Hmmm. I don't know. I've never seen one, but I wouldn't scoff at those who do. I used to be afraid of the dead when I first started my ministry, but I've gotten used to them now. They're not frightening; in fact, they're almost friends. They're so peaceful. Why do you ask?"

David looked out the window. "Well, I wondered in case I might see one what would I do?"

His father smiled at him. "A ghost won't hurt you if you don't hurt it. Just respect the dead and they'll leave you alone. Carry on as you would normally."

David nodded in agreement. "Yeah, that's what I was thinking."

By the fifth day of delivering *The Globe* to the graveyard, David felt more at ease. He never heard the ghost speak, since he now pitched the paper from the end of the laneway to the Beggs monument and ran. After two weeks it was time to collect his money. He had the usual problems: people not home, people with no change, people with other excuses. By the time he arrived at the laneway it was almost suppertime.

The graveyard was planted with great oak trees whose roots spread out, making the ground so uneven that David almost tripped as he walked up to the Beggses' plot. He waited a moment before clearing his throat and calling his usual greeting: "Collect. *Globe and Mail*."

It was so still, only the sighing of the wind among the headstones disturbed the silence. Beyond the church and the high office buildings that surrounded the graveyard, David could faintly hear the now comforting roar and honking of rush-hour traffic. He raised his voice and called out again, "Collect. *Globe and Mail*. It's time to pay." Minutes passed. It was getting darker and colder. Somewhere beyond the church a dog barked. David was shivering now. He cried out, "You have to pay. If you take the paper, you have to pay."

A thin, hollow voice rose out of the monument beside him: "But the dead don't pay." It spoke again. "The dead don't pay."

David felt his temper rising with the wind that was blowing around him. "But you have to pay or I have to pay for you!" he said stubbornly. He felt despair growing beside his terror as he said this.

The voice continued, "But the dead don't pay. We're dead. We don't have to pay."

David didn't know where to turn. Would he have to pay for Miss Beggs? An owl swooped past him, almost brushing him with its soft feathers. It flew to the bare branches of a nearby oak tree, where it hooted twice. Listening, David remembered Miss Beggs's declaration that *The Globe and Mail* started her day right. He remembered all the candies she'd given out at Hallowe'en since he was little; how she'd always top up the UNICEF boxes of every child with her pennies. He remembered his dad's advice to talk normally, not to be afraid of the dead.

Impulsively, he called out, "Miss Beggs, it's all right. You don't have to pay. It'll be my treat, my gift." He turned away in the cold evening and hurried home.

Was it the wind or the owl or indeed his dead friend — or his own imagination — that called out as he went down the laneway, "I couldn't exist without my *Globe*. Thank you, lad. You've made my day"?

David White went home and never told anyone that he paid the 1440 Yonge Street account out of his own pocket. One day, a few weeks later, the address wasn't on his route list. He wondered if Miss Beggs had decided to move on to a place where she didn't need her daily paper anymore. Later in the springtime, after he'd won his new bike and brought it home, some evenings he used to ride over to the graveyard and stop near the tall monument in the laneway. It was so peaceful there.

The Sealer's Ghost

Michael McCarthy
& Alice Lannon

Around 1875, when sealing was still an important part of the Newfoundland fishery, a man from one of the northern outports got berths for himself and his teenage son on a St. John's sealing vessel.

It was a long trek to St. John's to join the sealing ship, but the young boy didn't mind the hardships. Going to the ice was the dream of every young Newfoundlander of the time, and those unlucky enough not to secure a berth often went as stowaways.

They made it to St. John's and boarded their ship. With all flags flying, and to the cheers of the large crowd of spectators who had gathered to watch the sealing fleet leave, they steamed proudly out the Narrows.

The first week of the voyage was uneventful. After that it was hard and dangerous work, but the youngster did his part well, and his father was proud of him. Then disaster struck.

While getting ready to go over the side, the boy's father suddenly fell to the deck. When his son tried to help him up, he discovered that he was dead.

There was nothing anyone could do. The man was dead, but the voyage had to go on. As was the custom with death on a sealing ship, they wrapped the body in a winding sheet filled with salt, placed a cloth over the face, and poured a jug of rum over it. The body was then placed in a rough coffin, which was lashed down on the deck of the ship. The burial would take place on their arrival back in port.

For a day the boy was grief-stricken and mourned the death of his father. However, realizing that he was now the breadwinner of his family, he put his grief aside and threw himself totally into the seal hunt.

The rest of the crew watched as the youngster matched the best of them. There was no place too dangerous to go, and no load too heavy for him to carry. He was first off the ship at dawn and last back at dark. They nodded their approval, and said how proud his poor father would have been of him.

One evening, with a storm threatening, he wandered quite a distance from the ship in pursuit of a small seal patch. Intent on the hunt, he didn't notice the weather closing in until, having made his kill, he turned to go back to the ship. It was hard going, the swirling snow blocked his vision, the wind cut into his flesh, but on he trudged with his haul of pelts. The storm grew worse, and he wandered in a circle, coming back to the place where he had left the seal carcasses.

He began to tire and stopped again to rest, but he remembered his dead father's advice. "Never sleep on the ice," and he pushed on. But soon he had to rest again. Huddling in the shelter of some rafted ice, he felt the cold begin to fade, and a delicious sense of warmth began to steal over him. He started to grow drowsy but fought against it.

It was then it happened. Out of the swirling snow came the figure of a man, and as he came closer the boy suddenly started up, all sleep banished from his eyes. It was his dead father who was lying wrapped in salt in the makeshift coffin on the deck of the sealing ship. There could be no mistake; his father's features were clear and unmistakable.

He didn't speak or touch the boy, but beckoned with his hand for him to follow as he turned and walked head-on into the blinding blizzard. The boy stood up and followed him, trudging along behind the ghostly figure that kept close to him, but never let him catch up. When the boy began to falter, the figure urged him on, and he found the strength to keep going.

When it seemed he couldn't go a step further, the lights of his ship appeared through the swirling snow. He looked for the figure of his father, but it had vanished. He was alone on the ice.

He made it to the ship and was welcomed back as one from the dead. The captain and crew had feared they would have to report a double tragedy to the widow back home. When he told his story of how his father had come to him on the ice and guided him home, there were no disbelievers. These men had often heard similar stories of a dead loved one leading a person out of danger.

After he had eaten and was rested, the boy quietly went alone to the rough coffin lashed to the deck near the hawse pipe. Kneeling by it, he thanked his dead father for his loving care, even after death.

The voyage ended shortly thereafter, and the ship returned to St. John's. It was a bumper trip, and the captain, with the crew's consent, put aside enough money for the body of the dead sealer to be taken home for burial.

Needless to say, for the rest of his life the son tended his father's grave with loving care, and, long after the son's death, the grave marker told the strange story of his rescue on the ice.

The Mystery of the *Union*

Carole Spray

Jack Dyre was alone in his cabin aboard the *Union*. He could hear the waves scratching at loose rock on the shoreline, and once in a while, a seagull screamed, circled the barren masts of the schooner and then disappeared. It had been a long, boring day. The crew had gone ashore to visit their families at St. Martins, and Dyre was left behind to keep watch. He had walked the deck and watched for sixteen hours, and now he was tired. He wanted to go to sleep.

The seaman yawned and mumbled to himself, "There's nothing here to look at but the stars and the night and the sea. Time for bed."

He turned down the blankets of his bunk and curled up for a long, peaceful night. In the distance, the lights of St. Martins went out one by one, and the *Union*, tugging gently at her moorings, rocked slowly back and forth like a giant cradle. Soon, Jack Dyre was asleep.

It was just past midnight when a strange voice awakened

him. He sat up in his bunk and heard this command:

"Jack Dyre. Leave this ship."

Jack lit his lantern at once. He looked all around, searched below deck and above, but couldn't find anyone. Finally, he returned to his cabin.

"I must have been dreaming," he said as he rolled over and drifted off to sleep.

The voice awakened him again: "Jack Dyre. Leave this ship."

Jack jumped up, lit his lantern and made another search. But again he found nothing which would explain the eerie voice. It seemed certain that nobody was aboard the *Union* but himself. Nevertheless, his voice shook with fear as he repeated to himself, "It was only a dream ... only a dream ..." Soon, his head drooped down on his chest, his eyelids closed and he began to snore. But once again he was rudely awakened:

"JACK DYRE. LEAVE THIS SHIP." This time the voice was loud and angry and insistent.

It was more than Jack could bear. He did not bother to search. He didn't even bother to light his lantern. He just threw his clothes in a bag, fumbled around in the dark until he found the ship's companionway, and escaped from the schooner as fast as he could. The crew of the *Union* found him at dawn, pacing the dock at St. Martins. Shivering, pale and hollow-eyed, he clutched his seaman's bag to his chest and waited for Captain Kelly to approach.

"What in the name of heaven possessed you to spend the night here?" roared the captain.

Jack explained as best he could.

"Aw, come on, Jack. You've been having nightmares. We're sailing for Shulie this morning to pick up that load of lumber, and we need you on board. Pull yourself together, man!"

"No, sir. I won't," replied Jack. "I will never set foot on board the *Union* again. Never!"

"All right, lad, suit yourself," said the captain. "Bill Bradshaw is looking for a job. I'll hire him to take your place."

It was a beautiful clear day and the captain set sail at noon. The *Union* drifted on the tide for a while, steering for Shulie, Nova Scotia. She got partway across the Bay of Fundy, then stopped. There was no wind to carry her further. The *Union* and forty other ships waited in the bay, with their white sails reflecting on the mirror-like surface of a calm, unmoving sea.

The afternoon wore on, and Captain Kelly kept glancing at the sky, praying for a change in the weather. Clouds were gathering overhead and it looked like rain. But there was not a whisper of wind on the bay.

"Put on your oilskins, mates. It's going to pour!" called Kelly.

At that moment, the *Union* was plucked out of the ocean like a toy, and then she dropped, with her bottom up and her sails down. One of the crew had just stepped on deck when the schooner turned upside down. He leaped from the side and swam toward the ship's keel and hung on. Captain Kelly was trapped below in the galley. He forced open a hatch, dived into the companionway, which was under water, and then surfaced a few feet from the *Union*. The two men managed to crawl up onto the bottom of the ship. They clung together in the pouring rain and called out to their companions. There was no reply but the steady beat of heavy rain on still waters.

By early evening, the rain stopped and a team of rescuers rowed out to the capsized vessel. They took Captain Kelly and his mate to shore. The *Union* was pulled right-side up, towed to St. Martins, repaired, and safely sailed the Bay of Fundy for another twenty-eight years.

Whose voice did Dyre hear? And how could the *Union* flip upside down without wind or waves to turn it over? Nobody knows. The story of the *Union* is one of the many unsolved mysteries of the sea.

The Ghost Boat of Murray Harbour North

Teresa Doyle

A generation ago, forerunners were as much a part of life as birth or death. My parents and grandparents all experienced forerunners of one sort or another. Forerunners helped prepare them for the death of a relative or friend. A death sign could come in the form of a sound or a smell, the ringing of church bells, or the heavy aroma of a wakehouse filled with flowers. More often the forerunner was an apparition. The form of the dying person might appear to a distant friend. A sailboat sailing across dry land might stop at the home of someone about to die. An Island fiddler once stopped playing in the middle of a tune at a house-party. He saw three small caskets going out the window. A month later, three small children succumbed to the great flu epidemic of 1923. Their tiny caskets were passed through the window.

Perhaps the most common forerunner was a ball of light. The ball of light will hover over the home of a soul who was soon to depart this world.

Years ago, lobster fishermen lived together for the entire season. Every harbour had its own cannery, with a large cookhouse to feed the men. Sleeping quarters were on the second floor of the cookhouse. The season began on April 25, so the fishermen arrived at the harbour a day early with their mended traps, gear and new white cotton sails.

In the spring of 1936, on the 24th of April, the lobster fishermen were once more gathering to begin the season. By noon most of the men had arrived, and the air was alive with talk as they greeted each other and complained of the long, hard winter. The cold had not yet loosened its grip. The wind blew sharply off the land, the water was black, and the icebergs pushed up on the shore marked bright contrast to the dreary half-light of the day.

Toward evening, three lads set out to a nearby store to pick up some tobacco. The other men whiled away the hours in the cookhouse, playing cards and getting caught up on the news.

The lads were about a quarter-mile from the shore on their return trek when they spotted a fishing boat approaching from Murray Harbour South. The lads were quite surprised that someone should be arriving so late, and so they stood and watched as the boat approached.

The wind and tide had pushed a very large iceberg onto the shore, and the boat had to pass on the far side of the berg. Moments before the boat passed behind the iceberg, one of the two men aboard walked toward the bow to haul the big jib to windward. The other man manned the tiller in the stern.

From their perch on the rise, the three lads waited for the boat to come back into view and make anchor. The sailboat never reappeared. In a panic, the three ran to the cookhouse and raised the alarm. Not anxious to be taken from their card game to face the nasty weather, the occupants weren't easily convinced that the boys had actually seen something. Finally a dory was launched and the area searched, but nothing was to be seen. The wind blew hard off the shore, putting the far side of the iceberg in the lee of the wind. At the end of the berg where the wind from the shore whipped around the corner, the sea boiled with "squally water." The lads had assumed that the sailboat had gotten into trouble at this spot.

The men returned to the warmth of the cookhouse, and all the talk was of the apparition the three lads supposedly had seen.

Some time later the cook noticed a ball of light out in the harbour. With more than thirty boats anchored in a very small area on a dark night, it was impossible to determine which boat the light was from. Every man but one gazed at the eerie light. A young man, Dick Terell, one of the three lads who'd witnessed the disappearing sailboat, refused to look at the light, saying, "I've seen enough strange things to do me tonight. I don't want to see that light."

The next morning before dawn, the lobster boats departed. By noon most of them were back in port. In the early afternoon the winds picked up, and the men became anxious to see the return of the last boat.

Finally, just before dark, they watched from the cookhouse as the boat approached the shore on a long, sweeping tack. Seconds before passing from view behind the giant iceberg, one of the men on shore moved forward to haul the big jib to windward.

In horror, the men watched the scene unfold as described to them the night before. The boat disappeared behind the berg and failed to come back into view. In seconds the men were out of the cookhouse and had launched several dories. Rounding the corner of the iceberg, they saw the boat laying over on its side. The man at the tiller had managed to hang on. The other man had been moving forward when the craft hit the squally water, and he was thrown overboard. Within minutes they spotted him through the clear water, lying on the bottom. It was too late. Dick Terrell was dead. The unfortunate lad had witnessed the ghost boat the previous evening, and was the only man in the cookhouse who refused to look at the mysterious ball of light in the harbour, the light that signalled the approach of his own demise.

Ma Yarwood's Wedding Ring

Rita Cox

There is a old house in the village. Empty, weather-beaten and covered with vines, it stands on a large plot of land. The villagers say that that house is haunted, and they talk in whispers about what happened there, a long, long time ago.

The house used to be the home of Ma and Pa Yarwood. They had known each other since they were twelve years old, had married young, and were devoted to each other for over fifty-six years.

Pa Yarwood made a good living by driving rich people in his grand old Model T Ford, which he had worked and saved to acquire. He had looked after that vehicle with love and care. On Sundays, Ma and Pa Yarwood dressed in their best and went driving in style to the nearby town. The villagers were very proud of them.

The neighbours had great love and respect for the Yar-woods, and when Pa died, they looked after the grieving widow as if she was their grandmother, checking on her every day to ensure that she was all right.

Every day Ma Yarwood came to the village store. Her dark clothing, bowed head and shuffling steps did not obscure the strength, quiet dignity and determination that her neighbours had always recognized.

One day, a stranger whose name was Cyrus came to the village. He was talking with some of the village youths outside the store when Ma Yarwood came along. He observed the respect and deference with which young and old alike greeted this old lady. "Mornin', Ma," they called, and she answered, "Mornin', my children." He noticed something else, too. He saw that Ma wore a broad gold wedding ring on her finger.

"She must be rich," he said to himself. Then he asked the young men, "Who is that old lady?"

"Oh, that's Ma Yarwood. She lives in the big house up the hill. We have known her all our lives. She and her husband were always kind and generous to all of us in the village, but he died two years ago. They say that he left her quite well off."

"Does she live alone now?" Cyrus asked.

"Yes, she does, but the people in the village look after her and make sure she is safe and well."

Cyrus thought to himself, "I hope what they say is true. If she does live alone, it would be easy to break into that house. If she's wealthy, as they say, then this should be a good night for me."

That night Cyrus took a cab to the corner of the road that led to the Yarwood house. There were no street lights in the village; the only light on that dark night came from the flashlight that Cyrus carried. He came to the old house, climbed the steps and pushed the front door. It was open. Cyrus crept in. He went from room to room, searching through drawers, cupboards, shelves. He ransacked the furniture, looked behind the pictures on the wall, and everywhere he could think of, but found nothing of value to him. Angry and disappointed, he made his way quietly along a narrow corridor that led to the bedroom where Ma lay asleep. Slowly, he pushed the door. It creaked loudly, and Ma awoke.

Alarmed, she shouted out, "Who are you! What do you want!"

"Be quiet and stay where you are," said Cyrus.

But Ma got out of bed with surprising agility and rushed to the intruder, arms upraised, fists clenched.

Cyrus grabbed the old lady by the shoulders. "Stop screaming! Shut your mouth, or I'll kill you!"

Ma struggled and fought. Her strength and resistance surprised Cyrus, and he panicked. He placed his hands on Ma's throat. He squeezed and squeezed, until Ma fell to the floor, eyes staring. Cyrus stepped over Ma Yarwood's body. He turned up the mattress, he tossed things out of the dresser drawers, tore the wardrobe apart; he looked everywhere, but he found nothing. This journey was all in vain.

He turned to leave. As stepped over the old woman's body, the light from his flashlight caught the glint of the ring. He bent down and tore the ring from her finger, and rushed from the house.

On the main road he hailed a lone cab going to town. He climbed into the back seat. Cyrus was lost in his own angry thoughts when the cab driver spoke.

"What on earth is an old woman doing on the road at this hour of the night?" he asked.

From the light of the cab's headlights, Cyrus could see a bent figure walking slowly on the side of the road ahead.

When he came alongside, the driver stopped the car and called out, "Granny, where are you going at this hour?"

The old lady pointed ahead.

"Get in, Granny. I'll take you there." Turning to Cyrus, he said, "I hope you don't mind. We villagers look after each other."

Cyrus didn't answer. The old woman opened the back door and got in beside him. The driver started the car again and, as he drove, the old woman shifted closer and closer to the passenger. He crouched farther and farther in the corner. She moved closer and closer to him. Then the old woman reached out, took hold of Cyrus's right hand and pulled off the ring he had just stolen.

Terrified, Cyrus looked into her face. He took one look into those staring eyes, opened the car door and jumped out — right into the path of a vehicle coming the other way.

The cab driver stepped on his brakes, stopped the car and got out. The old woman had vanished. The passenger lay dead on the road, and the vehicle that hit him was nowhere to be seen. The police arrived. The bewildered cab driver explained the accident as best he could. "This young man jumped out of my car, into the path of an old car the like of which I haven't seen in years. It was a Model T Ford. It appeared as if from nowhere. It vanished as mysteriously as it appeared. There was an old woman in my back seat as well, and she too disappeared. These were strange happenings tonight. I don't understand it."

The neighbours in the village noticed that Ma Yarwood had not appeared in two days. They went to her house. There, on the floor of her bedroom, they found her, lying lifeless, eyes staring, her left hand clutched tight. They summoned the priest, the doctor and the village police. They pried open her rigid hand, and in it lay the broad, golden wedding ring that Pa Yarwood had placed on her finger over fifty years ago.

The Time of His Life

Rita Baker
(told orally by Ron Baker)

There was a time when I'd have said I didn't believe in ghosts, but that was before I met Ben.

My company was reconstructing a pioneer village, as a sideline, and I'd been assigned the job of locating an early settler's farm in Ontario, somewhere southeast of Algonquin, that we could buy and move to the village.

I turned off the road and drove along a rough track between parched, neglected fields, until it petered out in a desolate area of tall but sparse grass. The house was there, intact as far as I could tell. The barn was still standing, too. It looked like a good prospect. I wondered why no one had bought it. Not that it would be much use as a farm, with the thin topsoil just covering solid rock, but as a summer retreat it had possibilities.

There was no breeze to stir the grass, and the sun was hot as I stood on the stone slab in front of the porch. Pity they hadn't left a shade tree when they cleared the land. The boards sagged as I walked over them and through the open doorway. It was perfect — built of logs, weathered, but still firm. There was one large room downstairs, and steps up to a room under the eaves, with windows in the gable ends. Beside the house was a small barn, roughly made, which must have sheltered the pioneers while they were building their home.

The privy had collapsed, but was still enclosed by a fence. Somehow the sight of that privy made me realize that people really had lived there. I looked over toward the house, and if, as I said, I'd believed in ghosts, I might have thought I heard the rustle of long skirts and the clank of the bucket as it was hauled up the deep well. But I never was a very imaginative sort of fellow.

I found several interesting relics in the big barn: an old crosscut saw, harness equipment, a baby's rush basket. I jotted down the items in my notebook. If we could find the owner and persuade him to sell, the property would be valuable addition to our village. I turned to leave the barn, and there, leaning against the heavy door was a man.

"Hi!" I said, feeling unaccountably guilty. I hadn't managed to find anyone to give me permission to be there. He didn't say anything, just stood there chewing on a piece of grass and staring at me.

"Interesting place, isn't it?" I ventured. "You don't happen to know who owns it?"

He spat out the grass and straightened up. "They ain't selling, " he said.

"Why not? It's no use as farm land, and the house will rot if it's left empty much longer."

"No matter. They ain't selling." He sounded angry, and as he left the barn, limping, I had a nasty feeling he was going to swing the doors back and shut me inside. I hurried after him. In the hot sunlight outside the barn I saw that he was an odd-looking character — sideburns, beard … some kind of elderly hippie, I thought.

"If you would just tell me the name of the owner I could ask him myself." I followed him as he walked away from the barn, toward a clump of spindly pines.

"It's my place," he said.

So I explained about the pioneer village and why we wanted to buy the farm, but he wasn't impressed.

"'T'ain't right to come here and move a man's home. I cleared this land and built this home."

"Come on! This place must have been built back in the 1850s."

"1852 to be exact," he said, apparently unconcerned that he'd been caught out in a lie.

"You wear well for an old 'un," I said.

"I'm only fifty-six years old." The conversation seemed to be getting out of hand, and I was about to leave him to his madness when he grinned unpleasantly and said: "Here, I'll show you."

We walked around the clump of pines, skirting the heaps of smooth stones that had been cleared from the soil. He stopped by one of the heaps. It was set apart from the rest, and rectangular. He parted the weeds and pointed to a slab of stone. I stared at it, and a chill crept up my body, pricking my scalp as I read:

BENJAMIN CAMPBELL
BELOVED HUSBAND OF EMILY
WHO CAME TO AN UNTIMELY END
JULY 3RD, 1878
R.I.P.

"Emmie couldn't keep the farm going after I died. Always was hard work, even with a man around. Couldn't even afford to bury me properly," he said.

I looked at him and realized why I had thought him so odd-looking. He had a certain transparency about him. If you tried to look through him, you couldn't, yet the impression remained. I don't know what the norm is for ghosts, never having believed in them before, but if he was one, it explained a lot.

"You're a ghost?" I asked him.

He nodded. "Never could rest under that heap of stones. After Emmie left I couldn't bide the thought of anyone else taking over the homestead, so I sort of ... discouraged them. Doesn't take much to scare some folks."

"How did you, er, die?" I asked him, a little indelicately.

"Accident with the crosscut," he told me. "Bled to death." He pulled up the leg of his corduroys and showed me the stained bandages. I shuddered.

"Nowadays," he said, "I suppose I'd have been rushed off to hospital in a car, and I wouldn't have died. Didn't have many facilities those days. By the time we had the house and barn built, there wasn't much cash left for the things I needed to farm the land. Then when the drought came, we had to sell the cattle. Emmie never complained, but I knew I was a failure."

I had a sudden inspiration.

"Well, now," I said. "Wouldn't you like to see your house cleaned up, moved to good meadowland, and your barn in use again?"

I thought for a moment that I saw a gleam of interest in his eyes, but then he was angry again.

"Why don't you just go away and leave me alone?" he said, limping away over the field.

But, ghost or not, I had a job to do, with or without his consent.

"I'm going to try to negotiate a deal," I told him, as we arrived at a low grassy mound. There was a slope cut out of the earth on one side, with a door set in the bank: the root cellar.

I couldn't say exactly how it happened, but one second Ben was standing there by the door, and then he had disappeared. I think that was when I really believed his story.

I left the farm and spent the next few weeks tracing his descendants. I had a name to go on now. We found them eventually, operating a grocery business in a small Ontario town. They were glad to sell the farm, and once ownership was proved, I clinched the deal and arranged for a contractor to move the house.

Ben was as difficult as he knew how; employing delaying tactics, moving tools and causing disturbances, until Bayberry and Sons demanded an increase in fee. Ben didn't let them see him, but I'd find him in the barn or down by the root cellar, sometimes laughing, sometimes angry.

Eventually the house was on the road. I went back after I'd seen it safely escorted onto the route we'd been given. I think I was half-expecting to see Ben. I felt a bit of a heel about the whole thing, and was hoping we could part on good terms. But if Ben was here, he was sulking and wouldn't have anything to do with me.

I caught up with the house a few miles farther south. It had been delayed by a low-hanging hydro wire. Ben was there, of course.

"I get more seasick swaying along in that house that I did sailing across the Atlantic," he said. "But if I'm forced to choose between haunting the house or the land, I'll take the house. D'you reckon they'll set it down in a nice shady area? I always wished I'd left shade trees around the house."

I told him I thought it could be arranged. You might say I was squaring my conscience. I selected a beautiful site, near a creek, plenty of fresh spring water, shade trees, good grassland. We furnished the house and provided every piece of equipment a pioneer could wish for. I even had the privy reconstructed within easy reach of the house.

I had Ben's remains removed from the cairn and properly buried on consecrated ground, but it didn't settle him. He was enjoying himself too much. I still see him from time to time, smiling, running his hands over the objects he'd been too poor to own, or relaxing in the rocking chair on the front porch.

There's no doubt about it. Ben Campbell is having the time of his life.

Maximum
Nightmare

My Mother's Curse

Ted Potochniak

My mother was a mystic and a scamp. She read tea leaves for eager neighbours and she told me, her youngest son, stories with a "point." Now, you might think, "Ah, what a lucky upbringing, to have a mother who told you stories from the heart." Generally it was true. I loved my mother's stories — except those that had a point.

The story I'm about to tell you was just such a story, and it came about over a contretemps my mother and I were having about my going out to trick-or-treat on Hallowe'en at the advanced age of thirteen. Her final words to me were, "You're too old for that. It's embarrassing for the family. Your sisters stopped at twelve and so should you!" But I was stubborn and, besides, our neighbourhood was well known for its delectable homemade treats and the generosity of its people. Everybody, that is, except for old Mrs. Cripps, who had a penchant for dropping live house mice into our shell-out bags. I guess it was just her way of saying "Happy

Hallowe'en!" But she did serve a useful purpose, because we would direct any invaders onto our turf to her house by saying, "Go there first. You'll get a terrific surprise." It worked like a charm; our last view of them was always of a wild, panic-stricken rush through and over hedges after their treat bags were violently flung aside. I guess there's just something about a beady-eyed rodent leaping out at you with a peanut in its mouth that sparks those irrational, primordial fears lurking deep within all of us.

My mother and I continued our verbal sparring right up to the week of Hallowe'en. But then my mother uncharacteristically capitulated. She even offered to help me sew my pirate costume. I should have known better.

The day before Hallowe'en I came home late to find our kitchen plunged into darkness, except for a sputtering candle on the kitchen table. My mother was reading tea leaves for five neighbourhood women. Why it had to be in the dark I'll never know. You could have cut the tension in the room with a knife, because all of the fortunes my mother read were "unlucky"!

Then the tales started. I eagerly pulled up a chair. The stories fairly flew around the table, and I was drawn inexorably into a horrific web of tales of death, maimings and strange occurrences. At last, one of the women, Mrs. Bossy, said, "Bernice, tell us your family story of the 'curse of the youngest son.'"

"What?" I thought to myself, "I've never heard of this one before." I pulled my chair closer to the circle of flickering light. My mother's eyes got that half-closed, faraway look before she launched into a tale. I was hooked as my mother began:

The Curse of the Youngest Son

Well, you all remember how it was from All Saints' Eve to All Souls' Day in our village — the candles in the windows, the Masses, the prayers and the fasting. But then came the wondrous celebration of life in the town square — the dancing, singing and feasting that signalled the homage to the dead was over and it was time for the living. My father — you remember him, Olga — was a big, burly stonemason. Well, he decided he would treat the whole family to a night at the inn so that we would not miss one minute of the festivities the next day. All my brothers and sisters were ecstatic, but I was devastated. You see, I was still sewing my dress for my first dance. I was only thirteen and the youngest. I begged my father to let me stay home that night to finish the dress. It was, after all, my first real dance with young men who were not related to me, and I wanted it to be perfect. But my father was fearful. That night was a night for pranksters to roam, and it was the night of all nights for restless spirits to prowl among the living. The candles in the windows, you remember, were there to keep the creatures of the night at bay, for they feared the light.

I begged, pleaded and cajoled. My father hemmed and hawed. But my mother and my oldest brother, Longin, finally convinced him I would be safe. After all, our house had stone walls higher than a man. These walls ran all around the house, with high casement windows, and Machko, the family mastiff, would be on guard inside the wall to discourage any would-be pranksters. My brother even offered to come in the early morning to take me back to the town. My father reluctantly relented after my mother told him, "Your daughter is a young girl on the verge of womanhood. You must respect her wishes in this matter!"

Later I asked my mother why my father was so troubled. "Ah, your father," she said, "He's like all men — full of imaginary terrors when it comes to their daughters. They're worriers. They all have to learn you are growing up and embarking on your own journey."

At dusk they all left in the big wagon. At first I was nervous, but Machko's low growls and the sound of his claws pattering on the flagstones comforted me. I pulled the treadle sewing machine under the west casement window to catch the last of the sun's light, and began sewing.

All went well until the evening shadows inside the house lengthened and deepened. A curious sense of foreboding came over me. I shivered involuntarily. I lit some candles so that I could keep sewing. I had so much to do. But, I forgot to put candles in the windows. It grew darker — a darkness that seemed all the deeper in contrast to the weak haloes of the candles flickering on the sewing machine. A kind of evil chill crept into the house. Even Machko outside was affected. His growls were deeper and more menacing. Then, I heard footsteps crunching on the gravel road. Low moanings and keenings filled the night air. Machko barked furiously. I was terrified.

Then I heard, "Bernice, Bernice, Bernice, we are coming for you. We are the dead!" It was just some pranksters from our own village. I recognized their voices. One fool even attempted to scale the wall, but Machko's fierce growls and frantic leaps soon had them running for their lives. I went back to my sewing by the light of the dimming candles.

On into the dark night I sewed relentlessly, the only sound the whir of the treadle and the click of the needle through the cloth. But in the darkest hour of the night, I heard Machko growling and pacing anew. Had those idiots come back? On I sewed. Machko began to bay strangely. It was an eerie, nerve-wracking baying. He howled and howled. I could hear him leaping to the top of the wall. His clattering claws were unnerving me. I was about to go outside to quiet him when I heard him growl deeply, and then scrabble with his claws on the stone wall. What was troubling the dog? The last sounds I heard were the heavy thump of his body on the road outside. He gave a strange, gurgling yelp, and then a strange crashing, thrashing sound could be heard, like branches lashed by a powerful wind. All was deathly quiet again. Ah, I thought, he's leapt over the wall after some passing night animal. You all know how that dog loved the chase.

On I sewed. It was so quiet — not a sound. But then, that strange sense of foreboding gripped me again. Where was that fool dog?

On I sewed.

The chilling cloak of evil grew more pronounced. Even the air in the house seemed colder. I felt a menace from without such as I had never felt in my life. My breathing grew short and sharp. I could not even overcome the feeling of dread with my muttered prayers.

And then I felt terror — a palpable terror, a terror thick with evil intent, a terror that emanated from the high casement window above me. I wanted to look up, but dared not. I felt something, someone, staring at me from the window. But I would not, could not look up. It is nothing, I told myself;

just keep sewing and all will be well. The dog will come back soon. I felt a strange heat coming from the window — a heavy, moist heat in sharp contrast to the chill inside the house. I heard strange breathing sounds — guttural and sharp. But I could not, would not, look up. On I sewed. The feeling of dread grew even more palpable, heavy like a descending mist. It was then that the first drops fell onto my hands — a few, scattered, pattering drops. Something was there in the window. But I could not, would not, look up. On I sewed. The drops fell faster, like a burning rain onto my hands.

Something was above me. The breathing grew sharper, more menacing. The evil was real. It was filling the room. At last I could bear it no longer. I looked. There filling the casement was a huge, hideous visage with a long, lolling red tongue, and sweat was pouring off its grey, pale flesh — dead flesh, flesh that looked like clay from the river. The face thrust forward into the halo of light glowing from the candles. I heard a strange, blood-chilling scream. Then I screamed myself. In my panic, I thrust my hand under the needle just as I stamped on the treadle. The needle plunged into my hand and I fainted.

In the morning, Longin found me slumped over the machine. "Isn't that just like my stubborn baby sister — sewing until she fell asleep!" When he went to wake me, he stared in horror at the blood-soaked dress and the glittering needle impaling my hand. Carefully, gently, he drew the needle up and I awoke. I began to scream and thrash about, shouting strange things: "The face, the face, the face!" Longin was astounded. He ran to the old herb woman. She gave me some mixture to quiet me. I fell into a deep sleep, still muttering strange things.

Word was sent to my father. At noon, he roared into the village, bent on wreaking havoc on the rascals who had frightened his daughter out of her wits. All the young men of the village were brought before him. He ranted and raged, but to no avail. You see, they had gone on to the neighbouring village after their misadventure with Machko. But the villagers there had no patience for their tomfoolery, and they were all put in the jail for the night. They had all just returned that very morning.

What had happened then?

From my ramblings about the evil face in the window, they decided to climb up to it. There on the wet, wide sill my father found clumps of strange glowing hair. What was it? No one could fathom it. Longin then asked, "Where is Machko?" All the villagers set out in search of him.

Longin soon found him in our grove of fruit trees just outside the stone wall. The mastiff was straddled across the topmost branch of a tree. Longin climbed the tree to pull him down. How had that dog gotten up there? Machko was dead, his body stiff and cold. Longin kicked, pushed and pulled at him until at last the dog fell to the ground. They ran up to the dog — and then stopped in horror, for that huge mastiff had its throat completely plucked out. Its head lolled obscenely, held only by a scrap of fur.

My father called for the priest. The house was exorcised and I was anointed with holy oil. When I awoke from my restless trance, my father had all the young men brought to the house. Each in turn apologized to me for frightening me with their mask nailed on to a pole. When I asked about Machko, my father said, "Oh, fool dog ... he ran off on a hunt. Don't worry yourself. Come, Bernice, to the dancing. Look, I've bought a pretty dress for you!" I ran to my father and kissed him.

Later that week, the old *voroshka*, the gypsy woman, came to me. "Bernice," she said, "you have been visited. There was no mask on a pole. All the signs speak the truth. This thing will come back one day to your youngest son. It will come to him no matter how far you may stray from this place. It will come to him."

• • • • •

At this point, all the women turned to stare at me with their bright, black Slavic eyes. My blood ran cold. They said not a word. They only stared. I could feel the hair on the nape of my neck rise. Then there was an odd thump at our kitchen window.

"Teddy, go to the window," said my mother.

On nerveless feet I staggered over to the big picture window that overlooked the back lane. I held the cord in my numb fingers. Again came the thump.

"Open the blind!" shouted the women.

Involuntarily, I yanked on the cord and the blind flew up. There, filling the window, was a horrid face — a ghastly face, a face with a long, lolling red tongue. The face plunged toward the window. I screamed and fell to the floor. My mother picked me up and put me in a chair.

"What did you see?" she asked.

"Didn't you see it?" I shouted. "The face, the horrid face!"

"We saw nothing," they all said. "You're imagining things."

"Well, my little cossack," said my mother, "Let's finish your pirate costume."

"No!" I screamed, "I won't need it. I'm not trick-or-treating tomorrow. I'm going to church instead."

"Good lad," said my mother. "It's all for the best."

I never went trick-or-treating again. And, you know, to this day I'll never pull up a blind at night. You never know — maybe there was something to that "curse of the youngest son." Or maybe it was just a matter of having a scamp for a mother, someone who liked to tell stories with a "point."

No Pear-A-Bow

Cathy Miyata

In the prefecture of Fukuoka-Ken, out in the lonely country-side, there is a slope, a hill really, that divides the road. You could walk to the left and go around the hill, or you could walk to the right and go around. It would save a lot of time to leave the road and climb up over the hill, but no one ever does. It is whispered that No-Pear-A-Bow is there.

One night a young man was coming home from working in the rice fields. It was late and he walked along. All he could think about was his sweet wife, waiting patiently for him to return, holding a bowl of steaming white rice for him to eat. He walked even faster.

When he got to the fork in the road, he stood and sighed. He had so far to go. To walk around the hill meant another hour or more. He cautiously looked up the slope. All seemed quiet and undisturbed. The bamboo shoots rustled slightly in the breeze, and crickets shrilled their strange evening alarm.

"What could it hurt?" he wondered. He had never met anyone who had actually seen No-Pear-A-Bow. The poor farmer who used to own the land went mad long ago. Why should he believe the ravings of a crazy person? The occasional disappearance of someone from the village couldn't have anything to do with a hill ...

He stepped off the road and into the weeds that smothered the steep slope. Then he stopped. "Remember No-Pear-A-Bow," a voice whispered in his head. He shivered.

"This is silly," the man said aloud, daring the voice. "I am a grown man, with a wife and child. I should not be afraid of old stories and strange rumours."

Boldly he took another step.

"Remember No-Pear-A-Bow," murmured the voice as it crept up his neck, swirled around him and was swallowed up by the shadows among the trees.

He took a step back. He looked left then right. No one was about. He thought of his bowl of delicious, steaming white rice.

"I'll run," he announced bravely to himself, and started up the hill. As quickly as he could, he wound his way between the bamboo groves and bushes. It was more work than he had expected. About halfway up, he discovered a worn path and gratefully followed that.

By the time he got to the top of the hill, he was breathless and stopped to rest. The night was still. A sliver of a moon barely lit his way, but the path was easy to see. He stood and listened. Not a sound.

"How peaceful," he thought; but then he realized even the crickets were hushed.

He was just about to move on, when a sad, whimpering sound froze him in his steps.

"A wounded animal" was his first thought, but no, it began to sound more and more human. He leaned toward the sound, straining to hear it better. His eyes grew wide and anger washed over him, for now it sounded like a child.

"Surely a baby could not have been left here alone!" Pushing aside the bushes, he moved urgently toward the noise. Deeper and deeper, through the thick yabu, he thrust, until the sound was right beside him. Lifting the branch of a great pine, he paused and stared into the darkness. It was a woman! He could see her back. She was kneeling on the ground, her head bent forward so he could not see her face. Her hair was carefully plaited and wound up over her head. Her kimono, richly embroidered, spread out around her on the bare ground.

"*O-jo-san*," he whispered, trying to show his respect, for surely she was a woman of wealth.

"*O-jo-san*," he said louder, "please, what has happened?"

Her whimpering grew into a steady sob.

He dared not touch her, but obviously something was terribly wrong. He stepped around her to see if she was injured, but saw nothing that would indicate she was. She had her face buried in the sleeves of her gown and she would not look at him.

"*O-jo-san*," he said gently, "let me help you. I will take you down the hill. It is not safe for you to be here."

At this, her sobbing became a long, low wail and she pulled the sleeves tightly over her face.

He looked around uneasily. "Please, please," he begged, "we must leave this place. I will help you to get home."

She shook her head from side to side and screeched like a wounded crow.

"Stop that!" exclaimed the young man, for the sound was making his skin crawl. "Come now!" he insisted, "We must get out of here." Boldly he reached out and took her arms. He pulled her sleeves down, peering into her face — and gasped.

For what he saw was not a face. Where her eyes should have been, there were only smooth, empty holes. Where her nose should have been, there was only a slight mound of flesh, and where her mouth should have been there was only a pinkish bubbled blister.

He stared in horror as her face melted and moulded and shaped itself into an egg! A long, jagged crack appeared down the smooth slippery surface and an eerie moan howled from inside.

The man screamed. He stumbled backwards and fell heavily to the ground. The moaning grew louder. Terrified to look at her again, he turned and tore through the brush, scratching his face and hands. Wildly, he ran among the trees, tripping over roots and falling over rotting logs. Again and again he got up and ran, the wretched sound following closely.

Ahead, he could see a light. Like a moth, he ran toward it. It was a lantern. The lantern was attached to a cart. Miraculously, there was an *udon* seller! Someone was there to help! Almost blinded by his fear, he could just make out the pedlar bending over the wares in his cart.

Screaming madly, he ran to the figure and fell at his feet.

"*Kore, kore?*" demanded the *udon* seller, his voice oddly calm. "Tell me what has happened."

The young man lay there, panting and sobbing, struggling to find the words.

"Are you hurt?" the *udon* seller demanded.

"No ... no ... a woman ... a thing ... horrible ... horrible ...!" he babbled between sobs.

"What sort of a woman?" the pedlar asked, but the young man could not answer.

"Look at me and speak!" the *udon* seller shouted. The pedlar grabbed the young man roughly by his shoulders and hauled him to his feet. "Look at me!" he commanded.

By the light of the lantern the pedlar forced the young man to look up. Their eyes met. The *udon* seller gasped and pulled away. He covered his face with his hands, and stumbled backwards, falling onto the road. He looked up at the young man now standing over him.

"Ahhhhhhhhhhhhhhhhhhhhhhhhhhhhhhhhhhhhhhhh!"

And the light went out.

The Ugly Fox Fairy

Kate Stevens

Scholar Mu was a man of Ch'ang-sha. He and his wife were bitterly poor, too poor to buy winter clothing, though winter was fast approaching. Still, the scholar spent every evening in his cold, bare study, reading his books. He was determined to pass the Imperial examinations and become an official. Then, wealth and respect would be his.

One night he looked up and saw a young woman standing in the doorway. She was dressed in garments of glittering beauty, but her face was ugly. She smiled.

"You must be cold," she said.

"Who are you? How did you get here?"

"Why, I am a fox fairy who has taken pity on your cold and solitary state, and come to warm your bed."

Now fox fairies are very special creatures. After centuries of self-cultivation, foxes acquire the power to take on human form. They can help the mortals they befriend or, moved to malevolence, they can suck the very life-force from mortal bones. A fox fairy may be male or female, young or old — it all depends on their original fox form. Most young female fox fairies, if the stories we hear of them are to be believed, are beautiful. This fox fairy was an exception, with her ugly face.

The scholar was afraid of her because she was a fox fairy, and he detested her ugly face. He began to shout and holler.

"Go away! Get out!"

The fox fairy just placed a small gold ingot on the table. "If we can be together, this is yours."

Delighted, the scholar agreed.

The wooden bed platform in the study had nothing on it but a tattered quilt, so the fox fairy took off her silken outer garments and used them to cover its bare boards. They lay together until dawn, when the fox fairy got up to leave. "Use what I have given you to get fresh bedding made. There will be enough left over for good food and warm clothing. If we can be together always, you need never again fear hunger or cold." And then she was gone.

The scholar disclosed to his wife what had happened. She was as happy as he. That very morning she went to market, bought fabric, and sewed up a complete set of fresh bedding. That night the fox fairy came again. The sight of the new bedding pleased her. "Your wife is a hard and willing worker." And there was another gold ingot as a token of thanks. From that time on, the fox fairy never missed a night; each morning when she left, there was a gift.

A year went by, a year and more. The scholar refurbished and expanded his home. Master and servant alike went clothed in patterned brocade. Rare delicacies were daily fare. In fact, husband and wife lived like nobility. But gradually the fox fairy's donations grew smaller. Soon, the scholar detested her from his heart.

He sought out a Taoist magician, who wrote spells on strips of rice paper, to be pasted up on the compound gate, spells that would bar the fox fairy entry. When the fox fairy came that night and saw those strips of paper, she tore them from the gate with her teeth, gnashing them to shreds. Then she was inside the study. Scornfully, she denounced the scholar: "Faithless and heartless to the core! No power of mine will suffice to change you. Since you weary of me, I will leave of my own accord. But once the bonds of affection and loyalty are cut, all that you received from me comes due for repayment." She turned and was gone.

Terrified that she would indeed return, the scholar consulted the magician once again. The magician agreed to come set up his altar in the study itself, and perform an exorcism that would keep the fox fairy away forever. Everyone gathered around to watch as the magician set up the altar, placing on it the objects of magic and power. Suddenly, he doubled up and fell to the ground, clapping his hand to his ear. The onlookers saw blood flowing between his fingers, over his temple: his ear had been cut off! Everyone turned and fled for their lives; even the magician, still holding the side of his head, managed to scuttle away. Rocks big as baskets flew about the room, smashing the window lattices, the fine hangings, the rice vats, the vases. Nothing was left intact. The scholar cowered under the bed platform, curled into a ball, as sweat poured down.

Suddenly, there was the fox fairy, holding a strange creature in her arms. It had a face like a cat, and a large tail.

She set it down by the bed platform. "*Xi, xi,*" she said, "chew that faithless fellow's feet." The creature set to chewing at the scholar's shoes with teeth sharp as knife blades. The scholar tried to pull his feet into safety, but he could not move arm or leg. Teeth met bone with a crunching sound; the pain was terrible. The scholar pleaded for mercy.

"Give back all the gold and jewels. Hold nothing back," came the response. When the scholar agreed, "*He, he,*" said the fox fairy, and the creature stopped.

The scholar was too paralyzed with fright and pain to move. From beneath the bed platform he gave directions, and the fox fairy went to and fro gathering up the remaining valuables. There was some jade, jewels, and clothing, but only two hundred ingots of gold, which the fox fairy thought too little. "*Xi, xi!*" Once again the creature began to gnaw the scholar's feet. The scholar's cries for mercy resounded through the study until at last the fox fairy said, "*He, he.*" If the scholar would give back six hundred ingots of gold within ten days, she would consider the debt paid. Then she left.

It took a long time for the family and servants to return to the study. They found a room in shambles, emptied of all the luxurious fittings. Nothing remained but a old tattered quilt. They pulled the scholar out from beneath the bed platform. His feet were drenched in blood; two toes were missing. Covered with the quilt, he lay on the bare boards while the family bent their efforts to making up the required sum. They sold the bondmaids. They found a market for their own fine clothing. When the fox fairy came back ten days later, they hurried to press the gold into her hands. Silently, she took it and left. From that day onward never again did she enter the scholar's home.

It took six months of medicine and doctors before the scholar's feet healed. And the two of them, scholar and wife, were as poor as before. As for the fox fairy, she went to a neighbouring village, where a farmer, Mr. Yu, lived with his sons. He had been a farmer of modest means, but after the fox fairy had lived in that household for three years, their fortunes changed. A simple home became a mansion. Granaries overflowed with rice. There was gold enough to buy official posts for each of Mr. Yu's sons. Of the fine fittings that graced Mr. Yu's mansion, more than half had once been in the scholar's home. The scholar could only look on in silence, not daring to say a word.

One day the scholar, out walking beyond the village, saw the fox fairy coming down the road toward him. Immediately he went to the side of the road and knelt down, awaiting her approach. She stopped while still some little distance from him, wrapped five ingots of gold in a plain white cloth, and flung it in his direction. Then she turned about and, silently, went back the way she had come.

The farmer, Mr. Yu, died while still in middle age. Then the fox fairy left, although from time to time she would return to visit. And each time she did so, it seemed, some of the fine fittings in the home disappeared. At last the eldest son, one time when the fox fairy appeared, stood at a respectful distance, bowed and made his plea: "Our father is gone now, so you stand to us, his children, in the relationship of mother. You may not wish to take care of us yourself, but surely you would not want to watch us slip into the depths of poverty?" That time, when the fox fairy left, she took nothing with her, and she did not come again.

A Duppy Tale

Ray Gordezky

Once there was a boy who lived with his parents in a small house at the edge of a graveyard. One day he ran into the house and asked his mother if he could go out with his friends to shoot rocks at birds.

His mother said no.

The boy begged and pleaded, and pleaded and begged. "Please," he cried, "the other boys are already outside playing. They will leave me here if I don't come out soon. Please, let me go."

"All right! All right! Go out with your friends if you want, and shoot birds," said his mother. "But do not go into the graveyard and shoot birds there. If you do, you are sure to hit Simon Tutu, King of the Duppy Birds. Then you will be in trouble and I do not want to lose you."

The boy promised he would not go anywhere near the graveyard. And off he ran to join his friends. All afternoon the boys ran about, shooting rocks at birds. They did not hit any. But as the afternoon wore on, they drew closer and closer to the graveyard. They were not far from the entrance when the boy peered inside and saw, sitting on a branch in the crown of a tree, a beautiful and enormous bird. He could not resist.

Forgetting all about his mother's warning, or perhaps choosing to pay no attention to what she had said, the boy slipped into the graveyard. Quietly yet quickly, he drew a rock from his pocket and fitted it to his slingshot. He steadied himself, pulling the sling way back, took aim and let the rock fly.

Direct hit. The bird flew into the air with a screech, then fell to the ground dead.

Proudly, the boy ran over to take a look at the bird. But when he knelt down to pick it up, the bird began to sing.

"Why ya shoota me for?
Why ya shoota me for?
Mea Simon Tutu,
Why ya shoota me for?"

The boy was terrified and knew he was in trouble. He turned to run away, but got no farther than turning around when the bird sang again:

"Ya betta hurry me home.
Ya betta hurry me home.
Mea Simon Tutu,
Why ya shoota me for?"

To the boy's surprise, his hands reached for the bird and picked it up. He legs ran him home. As soon as he got there, the bird began to sing again:

"Ya betta pluck me now.

Ya betta pluck me now.
Mea Simon Tutu,
Why ya shoota me for?"

The boy's eyes grew wide and his mouth hung open. He did not want to gut the bird, but this was a Duppy, a ghost who was singing orders. The boy got a knife from the kitchen. He slit the bird open and cleaned it out. He had not finished cleaning the knife, when the bird began to sing:

"Ya betta roast me now.
Ya betta roast me now.
Mea Simon Tutu,
Why ya shoota me for?"

Beads of sweat formed on his brow and his face turned white as he carried the bird into the kitchen. Carefully, he placed it inside a roasting pot, put the pot in the oven and turned the heat up as high as it would go.

After a while the kitchen was filled with a wonderful smell, and the boy felt his muscles relax. But then he heard a sound coming from the oven. It was the bird singing again:

"Ya betta eat me now.
Ya betta eat me now.
Mea Simon Tutu,
Why ya shoota me for?"

Quickly, the boy turned off the oven and pulled out the pot. He reached inside. The bird was hot and it smelled so good. He broke off a small piece of meat and brought it to his mouth, knowing he should not eat it. He paused, and at that very moment the bird began to sing again:

> *"Ya betta chew me now.*
> *Ya betta chew me now.*
> *Mea Simon Tutu,*
> *Why ya shoota me for?"*

The boy bit off a small piece of meat and began to chew it. Oh, it tasted wonderful! Yet he knew if he swallowed it something terrible would happen. But he had no time to think about it, for the bird started to sing again:

> *"Ya betta swallow me now.*
> *Ya betta swallow me now.*
> *Mea Simon Tutu,*
> *Why ya shoota me for?"*

So the boy swallowed. It tasted so good that he ate up the rest of the bird.

He sat down on a stool, feeling relieved. There was no more bird. There was no more singing. And his stomach was full.

But … After a while, his stomach began to ache. Suddenly his pants felt too tight. He loosened his belt, but it didn't do any good. For his stomach was growing. It grew bigger and bigger and bigger until: POP. His stomach burst open.

Then from out of the boy flew the bird, whole again. It flew right back to the graveyard and landed on the same branch at the top of the same tree. Then it sang:

> *"Why ya shoota me for?*
> *Why ya shoota me for?*
> *Mea Simon Tutu,*
> *Why ya shoota me for?"*

The Wendigo at Widow Helferty's House

Joan Finnigan

Up on the Mountain Road, back in the days when some Aboriginal people still lived in the Ottawa Valley and the Irish were still flowing into the Gatineau Hills to take up land, there lived a very old lady named Widow Helferty. Widow Helferty lived in a little log house on a half-cleared farm high in the hills off the Mountain Road back of Aylmer, Quebec.

Now when she was very old, past ninety-five, Widow Helferty took very ill and, in true old-time fashion, neighbours began to call, bringing her chicken soup, homemade bread and apple pies. But then the strangest thing began to happen to all these callers.

Every time any one of them went in Widow Helferty's house, they were followed by a peculiar
click, click, click
all through the house.

Try as they might they could not locate the source of the
click, click, click.

They searched in the woodbox and behind the stove and under the bed. But the

click, click, click

could not be explained.

Then one day, Mrs. O'Shaunessy, Widow Helferty's neighbour, came to visit the log house. The odd

click, click, click

followed her into the house and then followed her out again, only stopping when she got back to her own farm gate.

On another occasion, Paddy Hogan from Hogan's Hill called on old Widow Helferty with some homemade hot-cross buns from his wife. The strange

click, click, click

stayed with him all the time he visited old Widow Helferty, and then the

click, click, click

followed him right to his front door, where he was met by his wife. Even his wife heard the scary

click, click, click,

which did not stop until he was inside his house and had slammed the door.

The story of the bizarre

click, click, click

in Widow Helferty's house spread far and near, and curious and noise-hunting visitors by the score began to turn up at her house. None of them, however, no matter how long they tried or how hard they searched, could find the source of the haunting

click, click, click,

even though it was here, there and everywhere in Widow

Helferty's house and followed her visitors down the road to their farm gates and to their front doors, going

click, click, click.

Finally, there appeared on the scene two young men who were ghost-layers. They listened very intently to the

click, click, click.

"We are ghost-layers," they said. "Leave it to us. We will solve the mystery."

They followed the weird

click, click, click

out the front door and then they opened the garden gate and followed the

click, click, click

all through the garden, and then they heard the weird

click, click, click

leading them across the fields, and they followed the weird

click, click, click

across the fields, and then the weird noise led them into the far bush,

click, click, click,

and then the weird noise led them through the swamp lands,

click, click, click,

and then the weird noise led them over the rocks, up the mountains, and into the Poltimore Caves,

click, click, click,

where the ghost-layers disappeared and never were seen again.

When the scary

click, click, click

returned to Widow Helferty's house, Alice Snowshoes, the wise old Indian of Aylmer, was called in to listen to the weird

click, click, click.

"That's a Wendigo," she pronounced. "Don't ever try to see it or find it. You can't. A Wendigo will never show itself."

The

click, click, click

at Widow Helferty's house continued until the old lady died.

Then the weird

click, click, click

ceased as soon as she was buried in the ground of the Mountain Road Cemetery and was never heard again in all of Western Quebec —

CLICK, CLICK, CLICK.

The Pack

Marc Laberge
(translated by Palomba Paves-Yashinsky)

St-Mathurin, a small village in the Appalachian Mountains of Quebec, was the scene of some very disturbing events in the 1930s. All the villagers became especially watchful. Three times in a row, the same series of things took place: there'd be an old couple, and the wife would die. Shortly after, the husband would mysteriously disappear, leaving behind no trace except for some animals' tracks, and broken bits and pieces of various objects. The neighbours were questioned, and rewards were offered in return for the least clue leading to a solution to the mystery, but all in vain. Nothing ever turned up. It was impossible to figure out; there was no apparent motives, no sign of a theft, no obvious connections among the victims, aside from the fact that they knew each other. There was no other evidence for the investigators to work on.

Finally the prime minister set up a commission of inquiry in an effort to shed some light on the affair. After a year had passed, the file was closed due to a lack of clues.

Then, on a particularly freezing night, Ligori Labrèche, one of the villagers, heard an unusual noise while attending to his best milk-cow, which was having problems calving. Curiosity lead him out in the frozen air to take a look. Off in the distance he saw a car hauling a trailer. He heard a sort of muffled, deadened sound, barking.

The next day panic gripped the village as the news of yet another disappearance spread. This one was just like the three others; no one had seen anything, impossible to understand, not a single clue.

Without quite knowing why, Ligori went to the village police station and told about what he had seen and heard during the preceding night. He also gave the description of the car and trailer. Without much enthusiasm or confidence, the police started to investigate.

In a neighbouring village even deeper in the mountains, the car in question was found on a farm. The farmer was an old bachelor, a likeable, hospitable and well-mannered man. Once again convinced they were wasting their time, the policemen asked him to come along with them for a few routine questions. During the conversation one of the investigators noticed that the man's ring was slightly chipped, and he remembered that a tiny fragment of the same colour was found at the scene of the second disappearance. They launched a second interrogation, and the man finally confessed. With astonishing calm, he cold-bloodedly told his story.

"For many years I've kept a pack of dogs in my stable. I trained them to hunt in order to survive, for I never gave them anything to eat. After a week or two of starving, when I felt that they were on the point of killing and eating each other, I would load them into my truck and drive them into the mountains ten or fifteen kilometres from my farm. Even in winter I would abandon them there and return to wait for them at my farm. They learned to manage, attacking game for survival, and the born leaders rose to the top of the pack. They were so starved that they devoured anything they came across, without leaving any trace. I don't know how they did it, but once they had satisfied their hunger, they always managed to find their way back to the farm. The strength and endurance of my beasts fascinated me."

The policemen now understood what had caused the loss of cattle on the farms in the region, and the depletion of the deer herds over the last several years.

"In order to have the dogs obey me," the old man continued, "I used to hang the leader of the pack by the neck. I would come back to release him at the very moment when he was almost totally suffocated. Of course, I lost a few dogs that way, but the ones I had taken down in time remained loyal to me 'til the end. They obeyed me blindly, no matter what.

"So I can now tell you that I am the one who went to the old widowers' houses. Each time I would bring my dogs in such a state of hunger that they were ready to kill in order to eat. I would ring a doorbell to have the old man come out, and I'd pretend that I'd had a breakdown or something. Once he was out, I ordered the dogs to attack, and I remained there until they had cleaned up everything perfectly well."

One of the policeman spoke up in dismay: "What astonishes us is that we couldn't ever find any evidence of a theft of money or anything else for that matter. You never stole a single thing. But if not to steal, *why* did you do this evil thing?"

"Long ago," the farmer explained in a quiet voice, "my father worked as a guide in these mountains. Two American hunters were found murdered, and it was my father who was arrested. He was condemned to be hanged. The four men who were really guilty testified against my father. But I knew he was innocent. You see, on the night of the double murders we were, as usual, poaching together near the Maine border. I appeared in court and told the truth, but nobody believed me. I was only a child, they said, and I was the defendant's child at that. They needed a guilty party, and besides, they were only too happy to get rid of a quick-tempered poacher. After my father's death we lived in misery. We were humiliated, obliged to move, even to change our name. My mother was so bitter and desperate that she died shortly after. For a long, long time I remained out of sight, swearing to settle my score one day. Yes! I did it for him, to avenge his unjust death. I did it for my father the woodsman, who walked freely and proudly on every trail of these mountains."

Very softly, in the voice of one who has always been sure of the motives underlying each of his actions, the old man added: "You are going to hang me. But this time, at least, you'll be hanging one who is truly guilty."

Badboy and Brother Mouse

Sharon Shorty

There was dim light over the summer camp that Grandma Carrie had set up. Inside the canvas tent, it was warm and the light shone through. The little ones were already sleeping. Outside, Tommy, the oldest grandchild, was busy helping his grandma. First, he carried in wood, then carried some water from the lake, and finally put some water in a kettle to boil.

Grandma had settled in at the table and picked up the moccasin she had been beading. Tourists were on their way through the Yukon, and she never seemed to have enough sewing to sell in town.

"Tommy, that tea just about ready?" asked Grandma Carrie.

"Just about, Grandma. Need anything else?" asked Tommy.

"Come here. I want to tell you a story."

Tommy finished fixing the tea and took it to the well-worn table. He brought two cups and a can of milk. He fixed his grandma's — strong black tea in a white metal cup. To it he added two teaspoons of sugar and a bit of milk.

168

"*Gunelcheesh*, grandchild. Now what did I say?" asked Grandma.

"Thank you?" said Tommy.

"*Anh*," she said, a reply that Tommy knew meant yes in their Tlingit language.

Tommy got his tea ready, three teaspoons of sugar, no milk. He went to get his sleeping bag and curled up on the makeshift couch, a chest covered with foam. This was his favourite part, just before she started. Tommy waited and wondered if it would be a Crow story, or one he hadn't heard of yet.

Grandma paused to sip her tea, then she began:

• • • • •

There was a boy at a brush camp long time ago. His grandma loved her grandson very much. She tried to teach him things that would help him on his journey.

One day the little boy pointed and yelled, "Look, a little mouse! I'm gonna catch him."

His grandma took his hand and told him no. She always tried to tell him, "Don't bother animals. Don't laugh at anything." At that brush camp after the moose kill, the people liked their favourite food, moose grease. The boy knew that mice loved moose grease. So after everyone went to bed, he sneaked around. He put grease on some brush and waited.

That mouse smelled it, see? And that badboy grabbed that little mouse. The mouse was just shaking. The boy said, "Gotcha, you funny-looking mouse! You have an ugly long nose!"

That mouse, he screamed, "Help! Let me go!"

No, the boy wouldn't let go of him. He shook him around, and he sang a song to that mouse: "Ugly mouse! I'm gonna singe your whiskers off! Stupid little mouse! What are you gonna do? Kill me?" Then he laughed real mean.

Oh-oh, that badboy shoved the mouse and put his nose in the fire. Badboy singed his whiskers and he just laughed hard.

So that mouse bit that badboy.

The boy cried to his grandma, "Oooow! Grandma!"

And the mouse ran away from that brush camp, crying, "Ooooh, I got no whiskers!"

So the mouse started his journey to Mouse Mother, the one who looked after the mouse world. Since he lost his whiskers, he couldn't find his way in the bush any more. Finally he came to a lake and saw his face. That mouse, he told himself, "Hey, where are my whiskers? That bad little boy singed them off! Mouse Mother, help me!" That little mouse was just scared. Just then Mouse Mother came. That mouse told her, "Mouse Mother, that badboy burnt my face! I got no whiskers."

"My son, you poor thing." She just held him.

After that, Mouse Mother decided to call all the mice of the world. Pretty soon all the mice of the world came to her. She talked to all those mice, maybe a million. She told them, "Look at brother mouse! Look at what has happened to him. He's been hurt badly by a human boy at that village down the river. Listen, you big mice, go get a big tree to carry the little mice in. You all go to that village. We will make them pay!"

But that little mouse yell, "Wait! Don't bother the old grandma! She gave the teachings of respect for animals. Let her live!"

So all the millions of mice were put in a big tree. The big mice carried that tree to the river. That tree moved so fast toward the village, they say it moved like a boat. That tree went fast, and pretty soon came by the big camp. The people of that camp wondered about a big tree moving down the river. Yes, those people got scared. They yelled, "Look, a big tree's coming down the river! It looks like a boat!"

Those mice must be strong. They carried the tree to the middle of the village. The big tree broke open and it sounded like breaking bones. The mice started to crawl out of the tree and onto everything and everyone. They crawled in their mouths, their ears, their clothes, and even in their guts! The people tried to get away, but there was too many mice. Millions of mice covered those people in that camp.

That badboy come out and scream, "Grandma! There're mice everywhere!" So those mice chased him. Some of the people tried to fight those mice, but it was no good. Those mice killed everyone in that big camp. Then the mice got back into that tree and went back in the river.

All were killed, except that old grandma, who brother mouse asked to be left alive. Years later, that old lady would tell this story about her old camp and her people. She would tell anyone who would listen, "That's why you respect all living thing, even one little mouse!"

• • • • •

Tommy sat quietly. It was quiet in their tent. The sun had gone down just a little bit more. He started a little smile that went into a full-fledged smile. "That's a good one, Grandma. I like that one. Can you tell me again?"

"Okay, grandchild, one more time. But I need another cup of tea. My throat got dry on that one."

Bonestories

The Corpse Watchers

Alice Kane

There was a poor widow woman once who had three daughters. And one day the eldest came to her and said, "Mother, bake me a bannock and cut me a collop, for I'm off to seek my fortune."

So the mother prepared the bread and the meat, and then she said to the girl, "Would you like the whole of this with my curse, or will you take the half of it with my blessing?"

And the girl looked at the food and she said, "Och, mother, there's little enough as it is. Curse or no curse, I'll take it all."

So she took it all and went on her way. And whether her mother cursed her or not, I don't know. But she did not give her blessing. The girl walked until she was tired and hungry, then she sat down by the side of the road to take her dinner. Suddenly an old woman appeared, all dressed in rags, and begged for some of the food.

But the girl said to her, "I've little enough for myself. Devil a bit will you get from me." And the old woman turned away, sorrowful.

175

The girl walked on, and toward evening she came to a farmhouse, where she asked for lodging for the night. And the farm woman told her, yes, she could have lodging there. But she said to her, "If you could watch the corpse of my son, who's in the next room, in the morning I'd give you a spadeful of gold and a shovelful of silver." And the girl said, yes, she thought she could do that. So the woman showed her into the next room. And there, under the table, was the corpse of a young man.

So the girl sat there until the dead of night, when suddenly the corpse got up from under the table and came over to where she was sitting and said to her, "All alone, fair maid?" And she was so frightened, she couldn't answer. And the corpse repeated, "All alone, fair maid?" And she opened her mouth, but no sound came. And he said to her a third time, "All alone, fair maid?" And still she could make no sound. So he touched her, and she turned into a grey flagstone on the floor.

Well, back at home the second daughter came to the mother and she said, "Bake me a bannock and cut me a collop, for I'm off to seek my fortune." And it happened to her just as it had to her older sister. She took the whole of the food without her mother's blessing, and she refused a share of it to the older woman on the road. And in the night at the farmhouse she couldn't speak or answer the corpse. And she too was turned into a grey flagstone on the hearth.

And then some time later the youngest daughter came to her mother and she said, "Mother, bake me a bannock and cut me a collop, for I'm off to seek my fortune."

And the mother prepared the bread and the meat and she said to her, "Will you have the whole of it with my curse? Or will you take the half of it with my blessing?"

And the girl said, "Oh, mother, your blessing please." So she took half the food and her mother blessed her, and she went on her way. And when she was tired and hungry, she too sat down by the roadside to take her dinner. And the old woman appeared to her, and asked for food. And the girl said, "I haven't much, but what I have you're welcome to share."

So the two of them took the dinner together. And the old woman turned away joyfully, but she said to the girl, "I'll watch over you. I won't leave you."

She too came to the farmhouse at evening and asked for lodging. And the woman said to her, "If you could watch my son overnight — his corpse is in the next room — in the morning I'd give you a spadeful of gold and a shovelful of silver."

And the girl said, yes, she thought she could do that. So the woman showed her into the next room, sat her down by the fire where the dog and the cat were already sitting, and she gave her apples and nuts and left her.

She sat there, and she looked at the corpse under the table, and she thought what a pity it was that so handsome a young man should be dead. And she roasted the apples and she cracked the nuts.

In the middle of night the corpse wakened up and came over to her and said, "All alone, fair maid?"

But she tossed her head and she said, "All alone I'm not! I've Douse my dog and Pussy my cat, I've apples to roast and nuts to crack, and all alone I'm not!"

"Humph!" said the corpse, "a girl of courage you are. But you couldn't follow me where I have to go."

"Oh, yes, I could," she said, "for I promised your mother I'd take care of you."

"Ah," said he, "but I have to go through the quaking bog. I have to go through the flaming forest. I have to go through the pit of terror. I have to climb the hill of glass. I have to dive into the Dead Sea. You couldn't follow me."

"Oh, yes, I could," said she. He tried to persuade her to stay, but she was as stiff as he was stout. And when he went out through the window, she went out after him.

He walked till he came to the green hills, and he knocked upon the green hills and he cried, "Open, open, green hills, and let the light of the green hills through."

And she said, "And his lady after him." The green hills opened and let them through. There before them was the quaking bog. As the girl looked, the corpse was already hopping from hillock to hillock across the quaking bog. And she didn't know how she was going to do it.

Suddenly at her side she saw the old woman of the road, only much more nicely dressed. She touched the girl's shoes with the wand that she was carrying, and they spread out several inches all round. And she was able to hop across the bog too.

When she got to the other side, there before her was the flaming forest, and the corpse already partway through. But there waiting for her too was the old woman, with a heavy cloak, all damp. She put it around her shoulders, and the girl ran through the flaming forest, and not a hair of her head was singed.

And in front of her now was the pit of terror. She could see blue lights. She could see snakes and toads. She could see many fearsome things, but she could hear nothing, because the old woman was waiting for her, and plugged her ears with wax. So she came safely through, not hearing the dreadful cries. And there in front of her was the glass mountain, and the corpse, already climbing up. But the old woman was there too, and she touched the girl's shoes and made them sticky. And she went running up the glass mountain as fast as he did.

When she got to the top, there he was waiting for her. He turned and faced her and he said, "Go home now. Go home and tell my mother how far you have followed me."

But she said, "No. I follow you wherever you have to go."

"You can't do this. Come and look." And he showed her down below them, a quarter of a mile below, the Dead Sea. "I have to dive into that," he said.

And she said, "I'll come too." And before there was time for another word, he dived right down, in the Dead Sea, head first. She jumped in after him without waiting a second.

At first, she was stupefied. But then she hit the water and her senses came back to her. And as she went down the water became green like the sky above her, until she found herself in a beautiful meadow full of flowers. And she was so sleepy she could hardly keep her eyes open. And she fell asleep with her head against the side of the corpse.

She didn't know how long she slept, but when she awakened she was in a bed back in the farmhouse. There watching her was the corpse — only he wasn't a corpse now — and his mother. They told her how she had saved him. They told her how a wicked witch had seen him and wanted to marry him, and he would have none of her. So she had turned him into a corpse hanging between life and death, until a girl could be found who would do just what she had done that night, and would break the spell and save him.

Now they asked her if there was anything she wanted from them. And she said yes, she wanted her sisters back.

So they were turned back into their own shapes again, and they went home to their mother. I'd like to think they were better, but I doubt it very much.

As for the girl, the youngest one, she married the young man. And if they didn't live happy ever afterwards, that may we do.

Saved by a
Syringa Berry

Merle Harris

Many years ago, a small Hindu sect left India because the custom of *suttee* (when a widow threw herself on her husband's funeral pyre) had been forbidden. After making many moves in an attempt to find somewhere they could continue this practice, they started a fruit farm on the outskirts of a mining community on what used to be called the Southern Rhodesia/Portuguese East Africa border, where I lived with my family. The patriarch, an elegant, elderly man whom we often saw in the village with his beautiful younger wife, had been ill for some time. Our African friends told us that he was close to death and the group were getting a funeral pyre ready for him, and that his wife was going to commit *suttee*. The rumour was rife, and my father, who was mine secretary, had the chief of police for dinner so they could discuss the situation. After much discussion, they decided that they had no jurisdiction over the small, independent community, and unless one of their members lodged a formal complaint, they would ignore the rumour.

Knowing this, a small group of children decided in great secrecy that it would be safe to witness this event. The pyre was being built in a cleared area, surrounded at a fair distance (at least a football field's width away) by wattles and syringa trees. We selected a good spot where we could hide in the branches of the trees and watch without being seen. When the old man died a few weeks later, we were organized. We had agreed to meet at seven o'clock when it was really dark and to make our way to our hiding spot.

There was a group of seven of us, aged from nine to thirteen, all equally terrified but not willing to admit it. We arrived, amazingly silently, and crowded together on a number of branches. We watched, totally fascinated, as four men, each carrying a burning stick, appeared out of the darkness and stood at the corners of the large wood pyre. They were accompanied by musicians playing the most eerie music I had ever heard. The widow, dressed in a white sari with a garland of flowers around her neck, led a small procession who carried her late husband on a litter, which was placed on top of the pile of wood. His widow removed her garland of flowers and placed it around her husband's head and stood back slightly.

By now we were, to put it mildly, petrified. The whole scene was surreal. The people, all dressed in either white or saffron-coloured clothing, appeared ghostlike. The sounds of the sitars, augmented by the mourners wailing and lamenting, was blood-chilling. Reggie, who was the most hyperactive kid ever known, started to get fidgety and quite stressed. His older brother pulled out a pea-shooter and suggested he use the syringa berries, which, when dry, are tiny and rock-hard, as ammunition to take pot shots to keep him occupied. The rest of us watched as the four men turned around, bent low and thrust their burning torches into the corners of the pyre.

The wood must have been extremely dry, as the fire took with great bursts of flame, loud cracks and snaps, and sparks leaping into the dark sky like shooting stars. Soon the whole perimeter of the pyre was on fire, and the corpse gleamed in the blaze. As the fire gathered in intensity, Reggie whispered that he could hit the corpse with the pea-shooter. Daring him to do so, and mesmerized by the whole scene, we watched Reggie lift the pea-shooter, load it and take aim. And then, in the utter darkness of our hideout and the brilliance of the funeral pyre, we watched in horror as the syringa berry sped through the air and hit its intended target on the forehead.

The corpse sat slowly up and looked straight at us! There was instant pandemonium as we all screamed and clutched each other tighter, except for Reggie, who, in the confusion, fell off his branch and went crashing down to the ground.

The noise from our group of terrified children outdid that of the funeral group, and we soon had a number of concerned adults around us. Some went to tell our parents and get the doctor. Others tried to comfort our hysterical group. Reggie, it was discovered, had broken both legs and one arm, and had to be driven to the nearest hospital, a three-hour journey. The rest of us, after much apologizing, were taken home, all too terrified to go to sleep, although we had been assured that the corpse was still a corpse. Fortunately, our parents thought we were already being punished as we all continued to have dreadful nightmares.

After a few days the hospital staff found Reggie more than they were willing to handle, and he was shipped home, his limbs encased in plaster. The six of us went to commiserate with him. Fortunately our village doctor was also there. He thought we had suffered enough and took pity on us. He explained that the sudden intense heat of the fire had caused the body's muscles to contract, making it "sit up." He also pointed out that it was physically impossible for anyone, from our vantage point, to have shot a berry that far, or to have seen it reach its intended target. It was our fear and overactive imaginations that had taken over when we saw the body move!

The members of the small Hindu community were extremely understanding and forgiving about our curiosity, and the fact we had interrupted and ruined their sacred ceremony. We never did find out whether the widow had intended joining her husband on the pyre. However, for years after, each time we saw her in the village, we would congratulate ourselves for saving her from a fiery death.

The Monkey in Disguise

Mariella Bertelli

Once there was a duke. He lived in his castle and there, living with him, was a monkey. Now, to have a monkey in that castle, in that town, in that country was very unusual, for monkeys did not live there. In fact the duke had received this monkey as a special gift from the king: that monkey came from a country very far away. For this reason it was much cherished by the duke and by all his court, indeed, by all the people of his dukedom, who stroked it and gave it treats and sweets, which the monkey much enjoyed. The monkey, for its part, had a gentle disposition and easily fit the role of mascot, in turn pleasing anyone who paid it attention, making funny grimaces and noises, turns and twists just to amuse, without ever hurting or biting anybody.

And so the monkey was allowed to roam freely not only from room to room, but also from house to house throughout the town, and everywhere it went it was welcome and treated well. But there was one particular place that the monkey loved visiting best: it was the house of an old, old lady, who liked the monkey more than most people because it often kept her company while she would sit for hours in her garden. Each afternoon the monkey would drop by, sometimes down a tree trunk, or slowly peeking its wrinkled face from behind a bush, always surprising the old lady and making her smile. The old lady became so very fond of the monkey that she would offer it candies and fruit, until one day she found out that the monkey particularly relished confetti, those sugar-coated almond candies that come in many colours. From that day on the monkey spent a great deal of its time with the old lady, who had an endless supply of confetti. And when the old lady became ill and was confined, first to her bedroom, then to her bed, the monkey continued to visit her and the old lady continued to feed it candied almonds.

The old lady was bed-ridden for a long, long time, and the monkey became her habitual and most faithful visitor. In fact, the monkey was an affectionate companion, unlike her own two sons, who appeared to be visiting their mother more out of self-interest than out of concern; for the two brothers were likely to gain a great deal in inheritance at their mother's death.

One day, the good old lady, consumed by both age and illness, died a peaceful death after receiving the last rite. The two sons swiftly organized the funeral and the burial.

The maids washed and dressed the old lady, according to the customs of the times, binding her head in fine white cloth and covering it with a pretty lacy bonnet. Then they dressed her in her finest gown, adding rings on her fingers and a gold chain with a cross around her neck. They finally adjusted her

BONESTORIES

hands together in a praying position. And she was carried off in the coffin.

Amidst this hustle and bustle, nobody had noticed that the monkey was in the bedroom, watching. For the monkey had been there from the start, receiving with gratitude a last confetti from the trembling hands of the old lady. The monkey had stayed on after its benefactress's death, watching quietly all the different rituals with interest and attention.

When all were gone, the monkey slowly approached the bed and there found strands of the binding cloth and other unused garments. Slowly the monkey began to wrap the cloth around its head, in the exact way it had seen the servants do with the old lady. The monkey then found a bonnet and put it on its head while slipping on the old lady's nightgown, all the while checking in front of a mirror, this way and that way, until it felt quite satisfied that it looked like the old lady herself. The monkey excitedly jumped around the room, making monkey-noises; it then lay down on the old lady's bed and quite comfortably fell asleep.

Soon after, the maids came back upstairs into the bedroom to clean up the room, but as they turned toward the bed they saw a body and thought that it was the corpse of the old lady. They had such a fright that they started to scream and flew out of the room as if followed by a thousand devils.

The funeral reception was thus abruptly interrupted. The two brothers went quickly upstairs to see for themselves, disbelieving completely what the servants had reported. They looked inside their mother's bedroom and they saw — the corpse? Was their old mother back from the dead to haunt them? The terrified brothers scurried downstairs and sent for the priest.

The priest arrived, followed by two altar boys with burning incense and holy water.

"Do not despair," said the priest, comforting the people gathered there. "This is the Devil's doing and, now that God is here, there is nothing to fear. I shall purify this house of all its demons." And saying this he sprinkled holy water everywhere, slowly proceeding up the stairs toward the demon-possessed bedroom. As the priest opened the door he was quite shocked to see that the "devil" was still there laying on the bed, impersonating the dear old dead lady. For surely it must be a devil, since the priest himself had just finished burying her.

Still, though afraid, the priest took courage, murmuring prayers and calling all the saints to his aid. He slowly approached the bed and the "corpse." He sprayed holy water over the bed, over the inert body, over the wrinkled face, when suddenly the monkey's eyes opened and its mouth spread into a wide full-toothed grin. The priest's knees trembled, his legs gave out; he was overcome with fear, temporarily petrified. Then he turned quickly, stumbled over the carpet and the two altar boys, and the three of them went head over heels, tumbling down the stairs, shrieking.

Servants, guests, priest and all ran out of the house into the streets, certain that death itself was after them. For the monkey rising from the bed had followed the priest and its company and had stopped at the top of the stairs to watch all the confusion at the bottom. The monkey by this time was extremely excited and had started to jump up and down, making quick, high-pitched trills with its voice.

A little boy, the son of one of the serving women, looked up while he was being carried out, and he alone recognized the monkey: "*La scimmia, la scimmia travestita*," he yelled, "the monkey!" And as the others also looked, they each in turn recognized the monkey, the monkey in disguise!

What had been terror one moment turned into mirth the next: everyone laughed until they had tears in their eyes.

As for the two brothers, their fear had been so great, as well as their guilt about feeling greedy at the moment of their mother's death, that they decided to donate, in her memory, a good part of their inheritance to the poor. And it was done.

As for the monkey, it was given a large supply of confetti to last it a lifetime.

John Tingle and the Old Woman of the Woods

Norman Perrin

Martha Tingle lived alone on a farm with her son, John, in the Ottawa Valley on Black Bay road. His father had been killed in the Great War overseas.

Martha didn't know if John Tingle was the laziest boy in the Ottawa Valley, but he sure had the competition on Black Bay road beat hands down. Each morning Martha would fix John a good breakfast of toast, eggs, sausages and tea. He would head out to the barn with the best of intentions, take one look at the manure piled up behind the cows, wrinkle his nose and head for the woods to pick berries. Berry-picking was the only thing he liked to do. Each summer Martha made dozens of jars of jam from the blueberries, raspberries, thimbleberries and chokecherries he gathered. He was always busy wandering in the woods, looking for birds and picking berries. There just seemed to be no time for him to chop wood, haul water, weed the garden, milk the cows and clean the stables.

Martha ended up doing all the work on the farm.

Now, this morning wasn't any different from all the others. Martha banged on the stairwell, and called, "Daylight in the swamp, John. Time to work!"

John Tingle got up, ate breakfast, headed for the barn, took one look at the wood, one look at the stable, and headed for the woods, where the air was fresh and the birds were singing. As he was picking some blueberries, he heard a strange birdsong that he had never heard before. It seemed to come from a dead maple tree nearby. When he went to the maple, he heard the strange call again, this time from a small pine. As he followed the sweet melody from tree to tree, he went deeper into the woods. It was late afternoon before he realized he was lost in the forest. As evening came, rain clouds covered the sun, and a cold hard wind began to blow rain through the trees, soaking John to the skin.

Night fell and a cold, wet, miserable John Tingle stumbled through the dark, looking for light. Where there is light, there are people. Where there are people, there are fire and warmth. And John Tingle wanted, more than anything, to get warm and dry.

He came to a small cottage and was about to knock on the door, when it opened, all by itself. Inside, John Tingle could see a lit fireplace, and on one side there was a bed. On the other side was an old woman in a rocking chair, rocking back and forth. The old woman stopped rocking and looked at John Tingle.

"John Tingle, John Tingle," she said, "why don't you come in and warm yourself by my fire?"

John wondered how she knew his name. He stepped across the threshold, and walked over to the fire. Soon he was steaming on one side, turning around and steaming on the other. All that time the old woman sat in her rocking chair, rocking back and forth, back and forth. Then she stopped.

"John Tingle, John Tingle," she said, "why don't you take off your wet, wet boots?"

John Tingle thought this was a sensible idea, and he took off his boots. The old woman came and took the boots, and put them in the middle of the room. She went back to her rocking chair to rock, back and forth, back and forth. And then she stopped.

"John Tingle, John Tingle," she said, "why don't you take off your wet, wet socks?"

John Tingle took off his socks and gave them to the old woman, who smoothed them out, folded them up and put them on top of the boots in the middle of the room. She went back to her rocking chair and rocked, back and forth, back and forth. Then she stopped.

"John Tingle, John Tingle," she said, "why don't you take off your wet, wet shirt?"

John unbuttoned his shirt and gave it to the old woman, who smoothed out the wrinkles, folded it up and laid it on top of the pile in the middle of the room. And she went back to her rocking chair, to rock, back and forth, back and forth. And then she stopped.

"John Tingle," she said, and she smiled. "Why don't you take off those wet, wet pants?"

John took off his pants, and standing there in his longjohns, he handed them to the old woman, who took them, smoothed out the wrinkles, folded them and put them on the pile. And she went back to her chair to rock, back and forth, back and forth. And she stopped.

"John Tingle, John Tingle," she said, "why don't you —"

John jumped into the bed, pulled off his longjohns, and threw them at the old woman, who caught them in one hand. She smoothed out the wrinkles, folded them up, nice and neat, and put them on top of the pile in the middle of the room. She went back to her rocking chair to rock, back and forth, back and forth. And then she stopped. As she looked at John he could see the red fire glittering in her eyes as she whispered: "John Tingle, John Tingle, give me your skin."

John Tingle took off his skin; it slid off him like silk. The old woman took the skin, smoothed out the wrinkles, folded it nice and neat and put it on the pile in the middle of the room. She went back to her rocking chair to rock, back and forth, back and forth.

And then she stopped and said: "John Tingle, John Tingle, give me your flesh."

John Tingle peeled off his flesh and gave it to her. She took the flesh, smoothed it out, folded it up and put it on the pile in the middle of the room. And she went to her rocking chair to rock, back and forth, back and forth, and then she stopped. John Tingle looked at her with big round eyes, as she said: "John Tingle, John Tingle, give me your bones."

John Tingle took his bones, *click, click, click*, and gave them to her. She took the bones, bundled them up and put them on the pile in the middle of the room, with the skull on top. The old woman went back to her rocking chair to rock, back and forth, back and forth, back and forth, until she fell asleep. So John went to sleep too.

In the morning, the sun was streaming through the window when John woke up. The old woman lay still in her rocking chair, fast asleep. So John got out of bed and went quietly across to the pile in the middle of the room.

I can't tell you how quietly he went.

He took his bones, and put them into place, *click, click, click*. He took his flesh and put it on, *slap, slap, slap*. He put on his skin, and it fitted him like, well, like a skin! Then he put on his longjohns, pants, shirt and socks. Picking up his boots, he tiptoed across the room to the door, which was still open. At the threshold, he bent down, quietly put on his boots, laced them up tight, and then he ran like hell.

He ran, and he ran until he ran out of breath. He looked about and realized he was on the road that led to the back of his own farm. He sped into the barn. There he filled the mangers with enough hay to feed the cows for a month. He milked the cows until they were as dry as dry could be. He cleaned out those stables as clean as a whistle.

When he was finished, he went to the kitchen, where his mother had just finished making breakfast. She didn't say a word when John came in, but put porridge, tea, toast, bacon, on the table. As John ate and drank, she went over to her rocking chair by the stove, picked up some knitting and she sat down to rock, back and forth, back and forth.

Martha Tingle looked at her son John and smiled.

From that day on, John Tingle was as good as gold, the hardest-working lad in the Ottawa Valley.

Will the Circle Be Unbroken

Jim Meeks

It was fall, near Hallowe'en, when Grandpa Mac died. The ancient Celts called Hallowe'en *Samhain*, and celebrated it as the first day of their new year. They referred to this day as the "hinge" of the year, the day on which the door between this world and the spirit world swings open, allowing free passage between the two realms. I had mourned the death of others, saddened by their passing, but my grandfather's death was my first experience with the heavy shadow of grief. The first time I had thought of and feared Old Man Death's inevitable visit to my own door some day.

Grandpa Mac's wake brought friends and relatives together from both sides of the family — the Baptists and the Pentecostals. The Baptists came with faces grim, looking stern and mournful. They brought food the womenfolk had prepared so that the family of the dead would not have to work in the kitchen. The Pentecostals came carrying food from their pantries and smokehouses. They brought musical instruments along to bid farewell with joyful hymns and sad lamentations. Some of the Meeks kin came with jars of corn "likker," hidden under their coats to avoid a sermon from the Baptists.

That evening Grandpa Mac's life, in the form of stories, was passed around among those gathered to sit up with the dead. Those who knew, loved and respected him told stories of wild encounters with government "revenuers" and with the law in general, of going up against the coal company's hired thugs, tall hunting tales, and his knack for making whisky.

When candles were lit and burning, my mother's voice rose high and lonesome, singing "White Dove." Others joined in, and it caused me to unleash an avalanche of tears. When I faced the horrible fate of crying in front of people, my father rescued me. He took me to the kitchen and let me sit at the table and cry. My mother looked in on us every now and then, but said nothing. My father sat in Grandma's rocking chair by the old cast-iron pot-bellied stove in the corner, rocking back and forth, back and forth.

Mother eventually came in and sat down across from me at the table. She took my hands in hers and said, "Sonny, I remember how you loved hearin' Grandpa Mac tell stories with haints and such. Let me tell you a story about a widder woman lived over yonder in Pelham." I pulled my hands away and wiped my eyes. I looked at my mother's hands, worn from constant hard work. They looked much the same as my grandfather's had. I looked at her face and saw age where none had been before. She began telling the story:

• • • • •

There was this widder woman lived over Pelham way. She lost her husband in the mines, and her little boy was her only solace and consolation in this life. People who met him thought he was a peaceable and sociable child, well mannered and respectful.

Once he ran off a-playin' in the woods, where he'd been told never to go. And didn't a big ol' rattlesnake up and bite him. Well now, he begun to cry out for his mother and she come a-runnin'. She beat that ol' snake dead with a hickory stick. She carried the boy on her back up to the house and done some doctorin' on him. But it wasn't nary biddy good she coulda done 'im. He up and died on 'er, and she cried so long and she cried so hard she thought she'd never be able to dry her eyes again.

One evenin' whilst she was a-settin' there in the rockin' chair like your daddy over yonder, that little boy's haint come right on in the room with her. She was a-settin' there, a-rockin' back and forth, back and forth. A candle on the table beside her was the only light in the room. The tears were a-flowin' down her cheeks in burnin' streams a-sorrow, and she was a-thinkin' about how much she missed her boy. And now his spectre stood right before her eyes.

He stepped up to the table and he picked up the candle, holdin' it up so as she could see him clearly. Then in a sorrowful voice he said to her, "Mother, please stop your cryin'. I can't leave this world and go on to my heavenly home because your tears are a-keepin' my clothes wet and heavy. Look at my buryin' suit." And as she looked, she could see that his suit of clothes was soakin', soppin' wet. She started a-wipin' away the tears, and when she took her hands away from her eyes, he was already gone from the room.

On the third night after that, the widder was a-settin' there in her rockin' chair, a-rockin' back and forth, back and forth. This time her eyes was dry and she was a-gazin' at a little picture of her boy inside a locket she wore close to her heart. Once more that child's haint come to her. He come right on up close, and picked up the candle, sayin', "Look mother, my clothes are almost dry, and I can already feel my spirit a-risin' toward my heavenly home." As she looked on, he slowly raised up from the floor and faded away.

She never did see her little boy again, nor his haint neither, but she kept his image near her heart. She was comforted to know that, by lettin' go of her own sorrow, her little boy's spirit had found peace, joy and contentment.

• • • • •

Mother stood up and walked over to where my father sat rocking. She walked around behind him and, placing her hands on the back of the rocking chair, stopped the rocking. She leaned over and gave him an awkward hug and a little kiss on the cheek, then she said, "James Arthur, why don't you come on in and join in the singin'?"

She came and took my hand and led me out of the kitchen. My father resumed rocking as we left. I think I half expected him to follow us and take my other hand, but he didn't. He sat there and rocked back and forth, back and forth. My mother led me to a cane-backed chair in the parlour, and sat me down. She turned and spoke softly to my uncle Billy. They faced the crowded room, and mother began to sing in her spontaneous free style. Uncle Billy accompanied her on the fiddle. Each of us gathered there added

"amens" and "hallelujahs" as we felt the power and spirit of
the music:

> Cold blows the wind to my true love, and gently blows the rain
> I never had but one true love, and in a cold grave she was lain
>
> I'll do as much for my true love, as any young man may
> I'll sit and mourn all on her grave, for twelve months and a day
>
> Now when the twelve months and one day were past
>   the ghost began to speak
> "Who is't sits there all on my grave, and will not let me sleep?"
>
> "'Tis I, my love, sits on your grave, and will not let you sleep
> For I crave one kiss from your clay cold lips and this is all I
>   seek."
>
> "My breasts they are cold as the clay,
> and my breath is earthly strong,
> And if you kiss these clay cold lips
> your days they won't be long."
>
> It was way down in yonder garden,
> sweetheart, where we used to talk
> That the first flower ever I seen
> has withered to a stalk.
>
> The stalk is dead and gone, sweetheart, never to return,
> And since I lost you, my own true love what can I do but
>   mourn?

> *"Someday we'll meet again, sweetheart, someday we'll meet*
>   *again,*
> *when the oaken leaves that fall from the trees*
>   *are green and rise up again."*

As they sang and played they were joined by others, including my father. When the song over, he turned to my mother and said, "Esther, how about helpin' me out on this 'un?" He launched into a rousing, foot-stompin', hand-clappin' rendition of "Will the Circle Be Unbroken?" that just about waked the dead.

Zinga

Jamie Oliviero

Long ago, in a certain village in central Africa, there was a young man and a young woman. They looked upon each other and both liked what they saw. So they were married, and in time they had a child; a little boy named Zinga, who was born laughing. Now, many things pleased little Zinga as he grew, but three most of all. He loved to press his head against his father's broad chest and hear the laughter rumble deep in his belly. He loved to watch his parents dance, for they were wonderful dancers and were often called upon to dance in celebrations in other villages. And most of all he loved the song his mother sang to him every night before it was time to sleep. It was a quiet little song with an African rhythm to it:

> *"Hush the child oh-oh-oh*
> *Mama say hush the child oh-oh-oh*
> *Mama say hush the child when the nighttime comes*
> *Or the crying will do what you don't want done."*

Now, one day Zinga's parents were invited to dance at a celebration in a village on the other side of the river. So they left Zinga in the care of his grandmother and set off to paddle across in their small boat. But halfway across, a whirlpool caught the boat and tipped it over. Zinga's parents were pulled underneath by the powerful current and they both drowned. But no one was watching, and no one knew what had happened to them.

Time passed. Back in the village, Zinga began to miss his parents, and he went to his grandmother for comfort.

"Be patient, little Zinga," she said. "Your parents will return soon."

But more time passed. Other people who had been at the festival returned to the village, but Zinga's parents were not among them. Again Zinga went to his grandmother, and this time she told him to fetch her divining bowl. He brought the hollowed-out gourd filled with rainwater. His grandmother gazed into the still surface, and using powers she carried deep inside her, she saw what had happened to Zinga's parents. Then she had to tell him. He cried and cried and would not be comforted.

But finally there were no tears left to cry, and Zinga asked his grandmother, "Bonne Mama, I fear I will die if I do not see my parents again. Isn't there anything I can do to bring them back from death?"

"Ah, little Zinga," she replied, "the dead are better left to rest in peace."

"But, Bonne Mama, they are my parents. I love them and they love me. Surely there is something I can do."

Unable to resist the young boy's pleas, his grandmother told him this: "Well, there is one thing, but you must be very brave. And even if you can do this thing and bring your parents back from death, what you see may not be what you expect."

But Zinga would not be discouraged. So at last his grandmother told him that to bring his parents back from death, he first had to go into the forest and peel a piece of skin from his body to make the cover of a small drum. "Then bring the drum to me and I will tell you what to do next."

So off Zinga went into the forest. He was such a young boy, but determined to see his parents again. He began to try to peel off a piece of skin, crying out for the pain was great. His cries awoke Turi the spider, sleeping in a tree nearby.

When Zinga told her what he was trying to do, she said, "What a brave deed for one so small! Do not cry any more, Little One. I will help you." Then Turi the spider began to weave a piece of webbing as strong and fine as a piece of skin. This she gave to him, and Zinga used it to cover a small drum. After thanking the spider he went running back to his grandmother.

She told him to walk along the riverbank, beat upon his drum, and after a time his parents would rise up to meet him. But again she warned, "The dead are better left to rest in peace and what you see may not be what you expect." But Zinga was not listening. Already he was running to the riverbank. When he got there, he marched up and down, beating upon his drum. As he played, the sounds of the forest seemed to join in. The wind through the leaves, the whispers of creatures in the shadows seemed to follow the drum beat and blend themselves into strange, unearthly music. Then Zinga heard a splash and turned around.

Rising up from the river were his parents. But the water had washed away all the flesh from their bones, and swaying there before him in the mist were two faintly glowing skeletons.

Zinga fell to his knees. "Mama, Papa, what has happened to you? Come back to me so that we can laugh and dance and play again!"

The bones of his parents rattled together and seemed to say: "We are tired, little Zinga. We long to rest with our ancestors in the cool mud of the river bottom. If you love us, let us go. If you love us, let us go."

Then Zinga realized what his grandmother had been trying to tell him; that the dead really are better left to rest in peace. So Zinga took his drum and threw it into the water.

This seemed to break the spell, and the bones of Zinga's parents sank back down into the river with a grateful sigh. All the bones, that is, except for one. As Zinga turned to go back to the village, lying there on the path was one gleaming shin bone — his mother's shin bone. When Zinga picked up the hollow bone and blew into it, a song came out:

"Hush the child oh-oh-oh
Mama say hush the child oh-oh-oh
Mama say hush the child when the nighttime comes
Or the crying will do what you don't want done."

All the way back to the village, Zinga blew into the bone and comforted by the sound of his mother's voice. And after that, he grieved for his parents no more.

A Dream-Time Story

Johnny Moses

· · · · ·

In my tradition from the West Coast, when the storyteller pauses, we must reply, "I-elth, we are listening," for the story to continue. "I-elth" is included to keep the original rhythm of the story.

· · · · ·

Long ago there lived a five-year-old girl. I-elth.

One night she went to sleep, and as she was sleeping she had a dream. I-elth.

And in her dream she dreamt of all her grandmothers and grandfathers standing in front of her. I-elth.

And one of the grandmothers approached her and started brushing her hair. I-elth.

In Indian culture on the Northwest Coast, when someone is brushing or combing your hair, they're cleaning your soul. I-elth.

So she felt so good when this grandmother was cleaning her soul, and she enjoyed this. I-elth.

And then the grandmother said, "Oh, you have such beautiful hair," as she was brushing the hair. I-elth.

Then she said, "Well, we must journey to our home now, the Other World. We must leave you." I-elth.

And the little girl said, "Oh, please don't leave me here." I-elth.

And the grandmother turned away and she started journeying to the Other World. And the little girl awakened from her dream. She was crying. I-elth.

And there in her bed, as she was crying, her mother was sitting next to her, brushing her hair, saying, "It's all right, you just had a bad dream." I-elth.

Well, night after night she began to have the same reoccurring dream, the same Elders standing before her and the same grandmother brushing her hair, telling her, "Oh, your hair's so beautiful." I-elth.

After a while she got used to this dream. Then she became a mother. She had one daughter and one son. Then she became a grandmother and a great-grandmother. I-elth.

She had many grandchildren and great-grandchildren. And as time went on she became very old. I-elth.

In the olden days the Elders knew when they were going to leave this world, and they would prepare themselves. I-elth.

And so, the great-grandmother, she approached her one daughter and her one son, and she said, "I must prepare myself." I-elth.

And that night when she went to sleep, that same night her daughter and her son, when they went to sleep, they found themselves in the same dream with their mother. I-elth.

But they did not recognize their mother, because, you see, their mother was only five years old in the dream. I-elth.

But when she began to talk in the dream, they recognized the voice of their mother, because, you see, the voice, the soul of a voice, never changes in a dream. I-elth.

And they observed everything in the dream. There were the grandmothers and grandfathers standing in front of the five-year-old girl. I-elth.

And the same grandmother approached the girl and started brushing her hair. "Oh, you have such beautiful hair!" I-elth.

And then, the grandmother said, "We must leave you now. We must journey to the Other World." I-elth.

She began to turn away from the little girl. And the little girl began to cry, and she said, "Oh, please don't leave me here." I-elth.

And the grandmother turned around in a full circle and faced the girl. So did the other grandmothers and grandfathers; they turned around and faced the girl. And they peeled off their old bodies. And inside those old bodies there were little children. I-elth.

And the one little girl grabbed the five-year-old girl's hand, and they began to journey to the Other World. I-elth.

When the one daughter and the one son awakened from their dream, they looked at each other. And they knew their mother had travelled to a safe place. I-elth.

And that is all.

About the
Tellers and
Their Tales

Rita and Ron Baker live at Dyers Bay in the Bruce Peninsula. They make a good team. Rita is a writer, and Ron a storyteller. Thirty years of storytelling, acting, clowning and miming in Canada have given Ron a repertoire of stories and a wide variety of styles of telling. Rita writes stories, plays and articles. She was editor of *Living Message/Anglican Magazine* for fifteen years. "The Time of His Life" was broadcast on CBC. It is Ron's favourite ghost story.

"We were camping in Northern Ontario with our four children, and we drove down a deserted lane. We came to an abandoned farm. Rita doesn't say that she actually saw Ben, but she felt his presence."

Mariella Bertelli is a writer and storyteller living in Toronto.

"It was the monkey in this story that first captured my attention. How could a monkey be living in Italy around the year 1520? This is when the story was written, by Matteo Dandello. He wrote it because he had heard tell about this monkey, as a real living animal. And now I am retelling this

story, because I, too, was intrigued by this monkey in disguise, a monkey that lived so long ago."

Michael Burns tells regularly at Hurley's Irish Pub in Montreal, and has been featured on CBC Radio numerous times. He tells traditional stories from the southwest of Ireland, including several stories from the *Fianniocht* (the *Fionn mac Cumail* cycle of stories). He tells his stories in Gaelic, English and French.

"I grew up in County Kerry, Ireland, and started my storytelling at the age of nine. My father and grandfather were both traditional seanchaís *(Irish storytellers)."*

Chris Cavanagh is a storyteller living in Toronto. He is also an educator, community organizer, graphic artist, puppeteer and poet — and a consultant in popular education, conflict resolution, organizational development and democratic leadership.

"'Ti-Flor and the Devil' is like my name: I do not remember learning my name and neither do I remember learning this story. My grandmother told me this story on those summers I would spend in Acadian New Brunswick. I would come home from picking blueberries and, if I hadn't already eaten my fill, I would have to help her cut green beans.

"Sitting on the porch, overlooking the most magical vegetable garden I have ever known, my grandmother would tell me stories of places that meant little to me as a teenager — mythical places and real places that she and my grandfather had been to. Much later I learned that Waltham was a place outside of Boston, Massachusetts, to which many Acadians migrated to work in the fish canneries.

"Later still I read of the remarkable history of my ancestors, from their arrival to and survival in Acadia to their expulsion by the English and their return to Canada in any way possible. I began to read the old Acadian folktales, and one day I remembered this story that I have called 'Ti-Flor and the Devil.'

"Much of the history of my Acadian family remains a mystery to me, and my memory of times with my grandparents is patchy at best. I have reinvented this story as best I can. My grandmother's name was Flora and so I renamed the heroine of this story Ti-Flor."

Rita Cox is an award-winning storyteller who has performed across North America, in Europe, Brazil and the Caribbean. She teaches courses, leads workshops and seminars, and performs for adults and children. Her stories have appeared in many anthologies and school readers. She tells stories from the Caribbean, Africa and around the world.

"There was an old house outside St. Joseph's in Trinidad. The people say it's haunted. My aunt Jane told me 'The Wedding Ring' about the house."

Gail de Vos specializes in telling stories for young-adult audiences. She delights in telling contemporary legends, trickster tales, Jewish folklore, family stories and local history. She teaches storytelling at the University of Alberta and for the City of Edmonton; she is the resident storyteller at Fort Edmonton Historical Park, and co-organizer of the annual T.A.L.E.S. Fort Edmonton Storytelling Festival. Her books include *Storytelling for Young Adults* (Librairies Unlimited); *Tales, Rumours, and Gossip: Contemporary Legends* (Librairies Unlimited); and (with Merle Harris) *Telling Tales: Storytelling in the Family* (Dragon Hill).

Teresa Doyle is a singer-songwriter with five recordings on her own label, Bedlam Records. "The Ghost Boat of Murray Harbour North" and four other ghost stories from the Maritimes are presented in song on her 1991 release *Forerunner*. Her latest CD is a collection of Celtic songs for children entitled *Dance to Your Daddy*. Teresa has performed in Canada, the United States, Europe and Japan. In 1993 she appeared with the Chieftains.

Her music is available from Bedlam Records, RR#3, Belfast, Prince Edward Island, Canada, C0A 1A0.

Joan Finnigan is a writer and folklorist who has sought out the stories, reminiscences, ghost tales, legends and lies of the Ottawa Valley. Her numerous books include *Laughing All the Way Home* (Deneau); *Some of the Stories I Told You Were True* (Deneau); *Look! The Land Is Growing Giants* (Tundra Books); and *Witches, Ghosts & Loup-Garous: Scary Tales from Canada's Ottawa Valley* (Quarry Press).

Cynthia Goh currently works as a scientist at the University of Toronto. She likes to tell stories about the island where she grew up.

"I grew up in a remote island in the Philippines, full of sandy, white beaches and warmed by the tropical sun — almost paradise, in fact, except that there was no electricity and there were plenty of 'manananggals,' at least according to my grandmother. I thank David McMillen for his help in getting this story written down."

Ray Gordezky was born in Los Angeles, near the edge of the San Andreas Fault. He lived through several major earthquakes, and a season or two of surfing at Malibu. He has had several careers and passions, including storytelling, gardening and consulting. He now lives in Richmond Hill, Ontario, with his family, and dreams of moving to a house by the sea.

"One day I was telling stories to a group of Grade 6 children who were attending a school in Whitby, Ontario. When I finished telling stories, I asked if anyone had a story to tell. Almost everyone turned to Kwesi Thomas and called out, 'Tell the duppy story!' Kwesi, a small, bright-eyed boy from Jamaica, didn't really need a lot of encouragement. He was standing beside me almost before I knew what was happening. I didn't know what a duppy was. He said it was like a ghost.

"He began telling his story in the rhythmic patois of his native country. The other children were smiling. They loved to hear him speak 'Jamaican,' as they called it. Soon he had us all laughing and chanting the duppy bird's words. When he finished, we asked him to tell it again. He did. When the other children left the room, I had him tell the story one more time. By coincidence, I had my tape-recorder with me. That was in 1993. I'm not sure where Kwesi is or what he's doing now. But I do know his story, as do countless others who have heard it and told it since."

Merle Harris grew up hearing stories in Africa and drew on this experience bringing up her sons. She has been telling stories professionally for fifteen years, relating traditional and personal tales to all ages. She particularly enjoys working with kindergarten to Grade 3 students and with senior citizens. She has recently started a Parent-Child Mother Goose Program for parents and babies/toddlers. She tells stories during the summer at Fort Edmonton Park, putting the human face on history. She is the co-author (with Gail de Vos) of *Telling Tales: Storytelling in the Family* (Dragon Hill).

Alice Kane is a storyteller, author and retired children's librarian. Her books include *Songs and Sayings of an Ulster Childhood* (McClelland & Stewart), with Edith Fowke, and *The Dreamer Awakes* (Broadview Press). She was a co-founder of the Storytellers School of Toronto, and has appeared at storytelling festivals throughout Canada and the United States. "The Corpse Watchers" is retold from the Patrick Kennedy story of the same name.

"Life is not easy. It holds sorrow and pain and disappointment, and long, grey periods of failure; but always, as the old stories teach us, if we meet the trouble squarely and come to terms with it and do the best we can, unfailingly we find that the clouds lift and the Beast becomes a Prince and new paths open

and new gifts appear. In my long life, as I look back, I am overwhelmed by the constant, steady proof of the truth of fairy tales. Long ago I used to tell stories every Friday to a class of boys at a downtown school. They loved Billy Beg and Lazy Jack and Little Fool Ivan and the Steadfast Tin Soldier. Sometimes they interrupted the story to advise the hero or cheer him on or warn the Wicked Baron that his doom was sealed: 'You old fool!' they'd yell, 'She's got the ring!' But as the story ended, they sat still and listened to the verse that closed it: 'The wedding lasted seven days and seven nights and the last was better than the first. I was there. They gave me brogues of porridge and breeches of clay, a piece of pie for telling a lie, and here I come slithering home today!' And that is true, as true can be. You'd better believe it — for success and joy and laughter and hope, birds singing and clouds lifted after rain, depend on your yielding to that joyful belief."

Marc Laberge founded the Festival Interculturel du Conte de Montréal. He has written and edited several collections of stories, including *Destins* (Québec/Amérique), *Le Glacier* (Québec/Amérique) and *Tout un monde à raconter* (Québec/Amérique). He tours throughout Canada and internationally as a storyteller.

Alice Lannon graduated from St. Bride's College before entering St. Clare's School of Nursing. She first published in the *St. Bride's College Annual*, and presently resides in Southeast Placentia, Newfoundland.

Chris Lindgren has been a full-time storyteller and musician since 1983. During that time she has travelled all over Saskatchewan and into Alberta and British Columbia to tell stories in schools and libraries and at festivals. She sings and uses a variety of instruments in her programs, including various handmade relics. Although most of her stories are traditional folktales, she has written many stories. "Moans and Groans" was originally published in a Coteau Books anthology, *Jumbo Gumbo*, and it bears some resemblance to Chris's childhood.

"My older sister Laurel used to make up stories constantly; some to scare me and others to entertain. I paid her all of my allowance in exchange for the stories I liked best, and at age ten, she was the youngest 'professional' storyteller I have ever met."

Dennis Mann discovers the stories of real life. His stories have been collected from the myriad people he has met in his travels.

"'The Other Way Home' came from a story told to me by a Grade 6 student in south Oshawa. He didn't want anyone to know that it was his story. Maybe, if he sees it here, he'll be proud of his imagination. I'm sure he has more stories to tell."

Mike McCarthy was born at St. Jacques, Fortune Bay, Newfoundland. After attending Memorial University of Newfoundland and Ottawa University, he taught at various Newfoundland communities, until his retirement in 1986. He has written a number of plays and novels, and co-authored, with Frank Galgay, several books on shipwrecks and buried treasures in Newfoundland. He is Alice Lannon's brother.

Louise McDiarmid is the co-editor of *Share a Tale* (Canadian Library Association), *Storytellers' Rendezvous* (Canadian Library Association) and *Storytellers' Encore* (Canadian Library Association). She has been telling stories to children, youth and adults for more than twenty-five years. She is an original member of the Ottawa Storytellers and a freelance storyteller. She has a background in library work and a strong interest in quilting, folklore, oral history and family stories.

"The germ of 'The Loup-Garou Ghost' came from a legend told by French Canadians living in upper New York State. I found it in an old black book of tales which accompanied a travelling

exhibit entitled 'Wolves and Humans' at the Canadian Museum of Nature in 1988. A few years ago I began trying to track down the book and the original legend, but, although I have found various retellings, I have not been able to find the primary source. I guess that is why I didn't protest too much when Henri got cantankerous and wouldn't go along with the original plot, and Albert dug in his heels, and they sort of took over."

Marie Anne McLean has been a member of T.A.L.E.S. Edmonton for many years. An avid painter (in oils), she sees storytelling as another form of painting word pictures. Since joining T.A.L.E.S., she has been painting word pictures in stories of small-town Western Canada. Her family and childhood provide her plenty of material, and in addition to telling her stories she also publishes them in magazines and anthologies. She has also performed on television and radio.

Jim Meeks is originally from Alabama. His stories are drawn largely from his own family and the rich oral heritage of the southern Appalachians. He often uses song and ballads in his stories. He is a co-founder of the Mississauga Dreamcatchers' Storytelling Circle and creator of Mississauga's "1996 Year of the Story" project.

Cathy Miyata is a storyteller, author, teacher and actress. Her book *Journey into Storytelling* (Tree House Press) is a textbook for studies in oral literature.

"'No Pear-A-Bow' has sparked more discussions regarding the ending than any other story I have told. I have heard many versions, and sometimes the creature is called 'the Mujina'. My favourite version I learned from Kikuko Hirayama. She says most Japanese children know the story and don't believe it ... until they get up in the middle of the night to go to the bathroom or have to walk home late, all alone from Juko

school. Then they know it is true. I like to tell this tale, using the age-old 'get quieter and quieter as you tell' trick. The scream at the end sends the listener right out of their socks. Then I blow out the candle!"

Tony Montague grew up in Notting Hill, London, a neighbourhood of great ethnic and cultural diversity. He studied French literature at university and tells a few literary tales, but the British folk music scene in the 1970s proved a stronger influence. One string of his bow is to rework old ballads — sometimes sung, sometimes told as stories. Another is to juxtapose stories on the same theme from different cultural traditions. Another is to integrate elements of drama.

"The origins of the story of Da Trang, which is widely known in Vietnam, are clearly archaic. It shares a common ancestry with the Greek myth of Melampus. Whether it began life in Europe and travelled to Vietnam, or vice versa, or more likely had its roots somewhere in between, is a mystery. I am convinced that this is a shamanistic story concerning the archetypal 'lord of the animals' — in essence the same figure as the Celtic god Cernunos represented on the famous Gundesrup cauldron, which dates from the first century B.C. I'm very eager to hear from anyone who knows related stories from other parts of the world about 'Talks-with-Animals.'"

Johnny Moses was born in a remote Nootka village on the west coast of Vancouver Island, and raised by grandparents who taught him the traditional ways. Of multilingual ancestry, including Nootka, Saanich, Snohomish, Dwamish, and Chehamus, he is a member of the Nootka and Tulalip tribes.

At thirteen he was given his great-grandfather's name, *Wistemini*, a storyteller's name meaning "Walking Medicine Robe." At eighteen he received his B.Ed. from the University of Victoria. He is an ordained minister in the Indian Shaker Church as well as a leader in *Sisiwis*, or sacred breath medicine. Johnny carries more than a thousand stories in seven Native languages.

"Stories are the sacred breath of our ancestors. Some people call our stories myth and lore, but we know they are the teachings. Each story contains many teachings. We never explain. We let each person receive the teaching they find at the time. Storytelling is to awaken the mind. It is a powerful way to teach children because it develops their imagination and different views of the world. Animal characters in the stories represent friends and relatives, so children learn about different personalities they will meet in their lives.

"Everybody has an important story. And a song is a release of that story. We take in poison daily. Through singing and crying, we release that poison. Everyone understands the language of the cry. Laughter and tears wash away poisons. So the stories heal."

Sheldon Oberman is a writer, storyteller and teacher in Winnipeg. He has written and directed plays and films, and written for radio and newspaper and songs with Fred Penner. His eight books include *The Always Prayer Shawl* (Penguin) and *The White Stone in the Castle Wall* (Tundra Books). His recent adult fiction, *This Business with Elijah* (Turnstone Press), is set in North End, Winnipeg. He travels widely, speaking as a writer and teacher and storyteller.

"How I found 'The Gift of the Dream Teacher' is as magical to me as the tale itself. I was adapting my children's book The Always Prayer Shawl *for the stage and needed my character Adam to tell a certain kind of tale to his grandson. I woke after a nap, recalling this story in detail, even to its source — the second-century Jews of Egypt. It fit perfectly. Yet when I looked for it in books, it had vanished completely! I could only find tales of its type — the instructive magician entrancing a foolish student. So I've subtitled it 'The Tale of the Old Wise*

Man and the Young Wise Guy' — not knowing which one I resemble more."

Jamie Oliviero is a storyteller and arts-in-education specialist. Over the past twenty-four years he has completed school residences in Canada, the United States, Kenya, Japan, Australia and Thailand. He has performed at children's festivals in Winnipeg, Saskatoon and Calgary. He has also appeared at the Winnipeg Folk Festival, the Yukon International Storytelling Festival, and on CBC radio and television. He lives just outside Winnipeg with his wife and two children.

"Some of the first stories I learned, as well as some of the oldest, come from Africa. It is the place where people first walked on the earth, and where they first told stories. 'Zinga' is a way of paying my respects to the storytellers I met, and the stories I heard during my time in Kenya. It is also an attempt to acknowledge the power and mystery that each human being carries inside."

Norman Perrin is a storyteller based in Toronto. He created and runs the Four Winds Library, a unique collection of storytelling books from around the world.

"Ever since I was born in the Ottawa Valley in 1953, I had been on the move in one way or another for twenty-eight years, never hearing stories at all. I wonder if they were chasing me all that time but never caught up until the Toronto Storytelling Festival in 1981. There I heard storytellers like Alice Kane, Paul Keens-Douglas (Tim Tim) and other wonderful tellers, for the first time. Since then, stories, their tellers and their listeners have become for me the wanderer's home. 'John Tingle and the Old Woman of the Woods' is dedicated to the memory of Janet Dolman, who helped point the way."

Helen Carmichael Porter's storytelling career began in her childhood, when she listened to family stories in the Ottawa

Valley and Peterborough County. Since then she has performed in hundreds of schools, churches and art galleries, as well as the National Arts Centre, St. Lawrence Centre, O'Keefe (now Hummingbird) Centre and Roy Thomson Hall; at the Tarragon, Factory and Blythe Theatres; and on national radio, television and film.

"When I was a little girl growing up in downtown Toronto, my favourite stories were the ones my older sister made up to scare me and my brother at night. We called them the 'David White' stories, since this was the name of their main character. In the stories, sometimes he was young, a Globe and Mail paperboy just like my brother; other times, he was a travelling salesman driving through countryside that resembled the area where my grandmother lived or where our cottage was situated. Of course, this made the story even more thrilling, since this familiarity suggested that the story might be true! We lived in an older neighbourhood in midtown Toronto, full of huge houses and trees, with nearby landmarks of a supermarket, a library, as well as four different church spires and an ancient graveyard that lay hidden behind one of the churches. My sister also wove these local landmarks into her tales, and, with her low, breathy voice, she stirred our imaginations so that we were not anxious to stir outside after dark. These stories were never written down, but I can remember the gist of them enough to include some in my own ghost-story repertoire. 'The Dead Don't Pay' is my version of one of those tales."

Ted Potochniak is a schoolteacher at Fern Avenue Middle School in Toronto. He has told stories often on CBC Radio with Tom Allen (on "Fresh Air") and Richardo Keens-Douglas (on "Cloud Nine"). He is an avid fisherman who has a cottage on one of Ontario's finest trout rivers.

Sharon Shorty is a storyteller, playwright and actor living in Whitehorse. She wrote her first play, *Trickster Visits the Old*

Folks' Home (unpublished), in a 24-Hour Playwriting Competition. She has been telling stories, her grandmother's and her own, at the Yukon International Storytelling Festival since 1990, using the traditional style, Tlingit marionettes and theatre. More recently she created "Sara and Susie," a comedic two-hander featuring two old Yukon First Nations women who are best friends. They tell old-time stories and make people laugh with their wry commentary on life in the Yukon. "Sara and Susie" has been featured on CBC-TV's "On the Road Again."

"I figure that my grandmother, Mrs. Carrie Jackson, may have told me about a million stories as I grew up. She lived in a small cabin in a small village in the Yukon. After supper, as she stitched her beaded moccasin tops by the light of an oil lamp, she would begin a story. 'There was a man ...' she'd start, and go on until it was bedtime. I can still see her complex hand gestures to show parts of the story and hear the different voices she had for each character.

"My grandmother was a storyteller up until her death in 1993. Even in the old folks' home, every time a nurse would come help her, she'd ask, 'You got time for a story? It's a short one.' An hour later she would be still telling her 'short' story.

"I wish I had the kind of memory that she did. Anthropologists talk about our rich oral traditions, and I've seen this firsthand. Remember, in the Yukon, contact with Europeans started just over a hundred years ago, and there are still Elders who can recall this. When I see how much my grandmother knew, it is overwhelming. 'Badboy and Brother Mouse' appealed to me because it was so theatrical. I adapted it for the stage in 1992, and our troupe played at the National Aboriginal Indigenous Games in Prince Albert, Saskatchewan."

Stanley Sparkes was born at Saunders Cove, Bonavista Bay, Newfoundland, in 1942. After his formal education at Glovertown and Memorial University, he entered the teaching field, where, as teacher and administrator, he became a strong promoter of Canadian writing, particularly Canadian educational materials in our schools and libraries. His leading book, *Search and Shape* (Glovertown Literary Creations, Inc.), has been listed for all academic Grade 11 students in Newfoundland and Labrador.

Carole Spray was born in Moncton, lives in Fredericton, and received her M.A. from the University of New Brunswick. She has worked as a teacher and assistant children's librarian in London. Her poems, stories and reviews have appeared in numerous Canadian magazines. She is the author of *The Mare's Egg* (Camden House) as well as *Will O' the Wisp* (Brunswick Press).

"'The Mystery of the Union' *is adapted from newspaper reports, manuscripts and log-books, although I heard the story as a child. I've never heard an explanation about why the* Union *flipped over the way she did, but there are stories of other ships along the Atlantic seaboard that were upset in a vaguely similar way. According to sea-lore, it was possible to 'buy wind' by throwing a coin overboard. Sometimes, if the coin was really a big one, the wind responded too enthusiastically and with disastrous results. Perhaps this superstition once formed a part of the* Union *legend, and was lost as the story was retold, but there is no real evidence to show that this is so."*

Kate Stevens heard her first Chinese storysingers/tellers while a graduate student in Taiwan, forty years ago. She has been fascinated by their art ever since. A fluent Chinese speaker, she studies with performers in China every chance she gets, and retells these tales in English. For twenty years a professor of Chinese literature at the University of Toronto, she is now retired to full-time telling and writing in Victoria, B.C., where she also grows an ever-increasing variety of Chinese vegetables in her backyard.

"'*Pu Song-ling (1640-1715) himself never qualified for an official post, in spite of (or perhaps because of) his brilliant mind. He lived out his life in the Shandong village where he was born, clerk to the gentry, tutor to their children. Pu's own comments, added to the end of the story, were: 'It is a brave and praiseworthy act to kill an evil creature at the moment it appears. Once you have accepted kindness from any being, whether human, ghostly or non-mortal, then you may not turn your back on that benefactor with impunity. If the scholar was truly determined on his course, no riches in the world would have turned him from it. Alas for the covetous one, author of his own misfortune.' He was fascinated by the out-of-the-ordinary: fantasy, ghosts, fox fairies, magic. Eventually he amassed a collection of more than 450 tales, of which this is one. His ways of collecting tales were diverse. He talked with fellow villagers, saved letters from literary friends who travelled. One method was peculiarly his own. He stationed himself beside the village well, situated at the foot of a steep hill. When travelling merchants paused to look at the climb ahead, he would say, 'Sit down and rest. The tea is free if you will tell me a story.'*

"*I love this tale for its ambiguity and its fierceness, and was excited to find it (it has never been translated, although many others have — see Victor Mair,* Strange Tales from Make-do Studio *(China Books and Periodicals). Pu made some of his stories up, seeing in them allegories for the injustices of his world. Knowing this, I cannot help wondering if just perhaps one day Pu asked himself 'What would ever happen if a young fox fairy wasn't beautiful,' and wrote down his own wonderful answer.*"

Ted Stone has been a full-time writer and editor for nearly fifteen years. His work has been published in magazines, journals and newspapers across Canada and in the United States He has published many books, including *Hailstorms and Hoop Snakes* (Fifth

House), which was a finalist for the Stephen Leacock Award for Humour in 1985. He has performed as a storyteller at a variety of festivals throughout North America.

Jim Strickland was born in Scotland and currently lives in Toronto.

"I learned 'The Piper's Tale' from a Scottish Traveller named Davie Stewart."

Dan Yashinsky is the founder of the Toronto Festival of Storytelling. He is the author of *The Storyteller at Fault* (Ragweed Press), and the editor of *Tales for an Unknown City* (McGill-Queen's University Press) and *Next Teller: A Book of Canadian Storytelling* (Ragweed Press).

"Before moving to Canada in 1972, I lived in Santa Barbara, California. The Ruins that inspired this story can be found in the Santa Ynez Mountains, north of the city. The house was destroyed in a forest fire nearly seventy years ago, and a child died in the fire. Whoever owned the land at that time had never tried to rebuild the house that once stood there."

Other Spooky Books and Audiocassettes from August House

FAVORITE SCARY STORIES OF AMERICAN CHILDREN
Richard and Judy Dockrey Young

Hardback $12.95   Paperback $6.95
Audiocassette (for grades K-3) $12.00
Audiocassette (for grades 4-6) $12.00

THE SCARY STORY READER
Richard and Judy Dockrey Young
with an introduction by Jan Harold Brunvand

Hardback $19.00   Paperback $11.95

GHOST STORIES FROM THE AMERICAN SOUTH
compiled and edited by W.K. McNeil

Paperback $10.95

TALES OF AN OCTOBER MOON
Haunting Stories from New England
created and performed by Marc Joel Levitt

Winner of Audioworld's Golden Headset Award
Audiocassette $12.00

CAJUN GHOST STORIES
performed by J.J. Reneaux

Winner of the Parent's Choice Gold Award
Audiocassette $12.00

THE TELL TALE HEART and Other Terrifying Tales
Syd Lieberman

An ALA Notable Recording
Audiocassette $12.00

CIVIL WAR GHOSTS
edited by Martin H. Greenberg, Charles G. Waugh, and Frank D. McSherry, Jr.

Paperback $12.95